SHOOTOUT

AT

RATTLESNAKE FLATS

A Clay Jared Western

R. Annan

Shootout at Rattlesnake Flats
Copyright 2016 R. Annan
WGA Reg. #R31889 (06.06.16)

Editor: Karren Doll Tolliver
Author's Portrait by Hazel Tertsakian
Photography © L. Annan

One Vision Publishing
ISBN: 978-1-942338-53-6 (Print)
ISBN: 978-1-942338-54-3 (eBook)

OTHER WESTERN BOOKS BY R. ANNAN

Fight for the Lazy M
The Red Bandana
The Gunfighter in Winter
Long Ride to Hell's Kitchen
Owl Hawks
Gunfight at Barfield Springs
Shootout at Sanctuary City
Last Days of a Gunfighter
Copperhead Moon
Cowboys of the Box R
Prisoners of Brimstone Pass
Range War in C Minor
Devil Wind
Showdown at Wamego Falls
Lightning Riders
Winter Kill
Gunfight at Wild River

In memory of the real Miss Ella

I miss you!

1.

The cowboy was riding from Colby to Atwood in the Kansas outback when he came across a campfire of three men. It was evening and he and his horse were tired after being on the trail all day. He welcomed the chance for company and idle talk.

The spark of light was a long way off when he first saw it down in a cluster of rocks beyond a field of whiskey grass and bluestem. A stream ran nearby where a big cottonwood reached for the evening sky. The place looked very friendly.

He could smell the coffee as he rode into the shelter of the boulders and shouted out to those inside, "Stranger coming in!"

There was a small, open area sheltered by a wall of stone where three men sat around a fire with their legs crossed. They were eating beef jerky and drinking coffee.

When they saw the cowboy, the biggest of the three stood up. Of the two still sitting, one was short and stocky, and one was as tall and as skinny as a picked-over chicken bone.

They all wore guns.

"Kin I help ya, cowboy?" the big one asked.

He shifted the cup of coffee to his left hand, then dropped his right hand down by his holster.

"Just passing through," the cowboy said. "I saw your smoke."

There was a coldness about them. Usually strangers were invited to sit and share. The cowboy suddenly realized that he had stumbled into a nest of outlaws. He slowly turned his horse so that it was broadside to them. Keeping the animal between him and them, he eased slowly out of the saddle to the ground.

"Nobody asked ya ta git down, cowboy!" the big one said.

The stocky one leered at the cowboy and said, "Kill him!"

"I can't," the big one replied. "He's a-hidin' behind his horse."

"Then kill the horse!" Chicken Bone said.

"I wouldn't do that if I were you!" the cowboy shouted out.

"Why not?" the big one asked.

"He's a cutter. Worth more than a thousand dollars."

The big one thought that over for a moment then nodded.

"Alright. You come out and we'll brace you fair an' square, then."

"All three of you?" the cowboy replied. "That's not fair. I'm just a cowboy, not a gunslinger like you all are. I don't have a chance against even one of you."

The big one turned to the thin one.

"You want him, Bob?"

Bob, the skinny one, shrugged. "Sure, Len." He looked down at the stocky one who was still sitting. "Unless Earl wants ta drill him."

Earl looked up at the skinny one.

"Naw, you go ahead and kill the damn fool, Bob," Earl replied. "I can't be bothered."

"Hell," Len said, "If you two can't make up yer minds, I'll do it."

"Can't you just let me go?" the cowboy whined. It wasn't a very convincing whine. "I got a wife and five kids."

"Stop yer damn cryin', cowboy," the big one growled. "An' come out here in the open or I'll drill yer horse!"

"I ain't no gunslinger," the cowboy pleaded. "Can't ya just please let me ride out?"

"Shut the hell up," the big one growled. "Yer makin' me sick ta my stomach! If ya ain't out in three seconds yer horse an' you is both gonna git lead poison."

"Alright, alright!" the cowboy whined again. "I'm coming out!"

He walked slowly around and away from his horse with his hand down by his Colt.

"What's yer name?" the big man asked.

"Why?"

"Because when I tell about it I wanna say who I drilled, thet's why, ya damn fool."

Suddenly the cowboy smiled.

"My name is Clay Jared, you damn fool!"

Jared's hand became a blur as he drew and fanned off three shots. Bob, Len and Earl drew, too, but fired off target as Jared moved sideways.

The big man called Len grunted as Jared's first bullet slammed into his chest, knocking him flat on his back. Jared's second and third bullets took Bob and Earl in their hearts, slamming them up against the rocks. They sat there a moment with a puzzled look on their faces and then toppled sideways.

As Jared reloaded his Colt he felt a pain and a warm wetness and realized that one of the outlaws' bullets had bounced off a rock and hit him low in his back. It hadn't gone through, but just deep enough to stay in.

Jared took a roll of cotton cloth from a medicine box in his saddlebag and wrapped it around his waist several times to cover the hole where the bullet was. This seemed to stop the bleeding. The wound slowed him down a bit as he dragged the bodies to one side.

Finally, he threw his saddle and bedroll by the fire and got a tin cup from his saddlebag. He filled it with coffee and sat drinking until he started to doze off from exhaustion and strain. With a bullet in his back, it was hard to find a sleeping position. In the end, he fell asleep on his stomach.

He awoke at sunrise, had a quick breakfast of beef jerky, hardtack and coffee, then went through the saddlebags of the dead men. He discovered a bag of money that had Rattlesnake Flats Savings and Loan stenciled on it in red letters. He had passed through the Flats once, a long, long time ago. It was a small cattle town near the Beaver River. Herds coming up from Texas stopped there to water. The cowboys usually went into town to spend money on the way to the railhead in Atwood City. Coming back, they had more to spend.

Jared sat down and counted the money. All told it came to $30,000, mostly paper bills. He put the money in his saddlebag.

He tried to think if Rattlesnake Flats had a doctor or not, but couldn't recall.

2.

Clay Jared rode slowly into Rattlesnake Flats towing three horses behind him. Each horse had a body tied across the saddle.

Anyone who knew horses knew that Jared was a cowboy because he was riding a quarter horse. They would also know that the three mustangs behind him with the bodies were outlaw horses, known for their endurance. Therefore, Jared was probably a cowboy turned bounty hunter.

People stopped to stare at this unusual sight, curious as to who this stranger was. A few people followed along behind him, wondering what he was up to. He nodded to them. A young boy ran ahead to tell the marshal. Jared saw him go into the jailhouse down the road.

By the time Jared got there, the marshal, a thin, old, gray-haired man, had come out on the jailhouse porch to take a look. He'd quickly sized the situation up.

"You a bounty hunter, sonny?"

Jared chuckled. He hadn't been called 'sonny' since he was a young boy, some years ago.

"Yeah," Jared replied. Being taken for a bounty hunter seemed more impressive than being taken for a plain, on-the-drift cowboy. "Jared. Clay Jared."

"I'm Marshal Nelson. Aaron Nelson."

The marshal walked over to examine the bodies.

"You did this all by yerself?" he asked.

"Yep," Jared said as he dismounted. He pulled the sack of money from the saddlebag and handed it to the marshal. The marshal stared at it for a moment and nodded. "Thirty-thousand. I suspect there's a reward, maybe?" Jared asked.

The marshal nodded. "Yep. Five hundred fer the money, an' five hundred fer bringin' in the robbers."

"A thousand?"

"Thet's right. A thousand," the marshal said. Jared whistled. He suddenly felt rich. "Let's get these bodies over to Uriah Freed's place. He's the one who plants 'em."

"Good idea," Jared said, "they're starting to smell."

Jared tied his horse to the rail and followed the marshal down the road, towing the three outlaw mounts behind him.

"After we drop off the bodies, we'll figure out how ta divvy up the rest," the marshal said. "Thet's usually what I do."

"How do you work it?" Jared asked later, as they walked back to the jailhouse with the horses. He noticed the old man walked with a limp in his left leg, most likely from a gun wound.

"When we git inside, I'll explain it to ya," the marshal said.

Five minutes later they were sitting at the marshal's desk in the jailhouse going over the figures.

"Here's how we do it, sonny," the marshal said. "You git ta keep the horses, saddles and all the rest of the stuff, including the guns an' rifles. But ya have ta reimburse the undertaker fer the boxes an' the burial."

"How much is that?"

"Well, the three boxes will cost twelve dollars, and the diggin' and burials will cost ya twenty-seven dollars."

Jared thought about it for a moment.

"What should I do with the horses and stuff?"

The old marshal scratched his whiskers and screwed up his forehead in contemplation.

"Wal, if I was in yer boots, I'd take the mustangs down to Tom Sloan. Let him sell them. Of course, he'll want a forty-percent take."

"Who's Tom Sloan?"

"He's the town blacksmith. An' he owns the stables, too. Like I said, he'll want forty percent."

"Okay, what about the saddles, rifles and stuff?"

"I'd take thet stuff all over to Gil Baxter."

"Who's Gil Baxter?"

"He owns the mercantile. He'll want thirty percent fer sellin' it fer ya."

Jared chuckled. The percentages were pretty high, but then it was all profit on his part. He would make a pretty penny if it was all sold. The mustangs alone would bring him nearly a thousand dollars, and the three saddles, bridles, saddlebags and rifles would net him close to another thousand.

He could leave Rattlesnake Flats with thousands of dollars! With that kind of money, he could be his own boss for a long time before he had to go back to work.

"Help me out with this, Marshal," Jared said, "and I'll let you have ten percent on all sales."

"No need to, sonny," the marshal said. "You saved me a heck of a lot of trouble by bringin' these hombres in. The town council was on my back like stink on a skunk. Now it don't need no doin'."

"Nevertheless," Jared insisted. "You get ten percent."

"Alright. Thanks, I kin sure use it," the marshal said. He reached out and shook Jared's hand.

Jared took an instant liking to the old man.

"Your limp? I noticed."

"Yeah. I was a cowboy as a youngster, then rode with the Texas Rangers fer a spell until I got winged in tha leg."

"You have my respect, Marshal."

"An' you got mine, Jared," Marshal Nelson replied. He thought for a moment, then said, "I reckon the first move is ta git the money back ta the bank and see the looks on their faces. Come on."

They walked up the road to the Rattlesnake Flats Savings and Loan, a small frame building next to Della's Beanery and Boarding House.

The bank manager was an elderly, distinguished looking man named Otis Jensen. He and his wife Marsha, who worked as a teller, were the only two people who operated the bank. After counting the money, they thanked him up and down and handed him an envelope with five one hundred dollar bills.

They also gave him another envelope with another five hundred dollars from the town council. One reward was for the return of the money and the other was for the apprehension of the robbers, dead or alive.

"The whole town donated money, Mr. Jared," Mrs. Jensen said in a happy voice. "Especially Mr. Zanuck. He's such a lovely man."

Jared smiled and nodded. He almost felt guilty for taking the money. Mrs. Jenson was such a sweet person.

After the bank, they settled the business of dropping the horses off with the blacksmith, Tom Sloan, and then the saddles, rifles and other gear at the mercantile with Gil Baxter.

Outside on the street, Jared said, "Is there a doc in town?"

The marshal chuckled. "There sure is, Doc Goodwin. The best sawbones around. Why, ya feelin' sick?"

"I got a bullet in my back," Jared said. "It's starting to rattle me a little."

"Jesus! Why didn't ya tell me before, sonny! Let's go!"

The doctor's place was across the street from the jail, but a little further down. As they walked along, the marshal talked.

"If yer lookin' ta settle down, sonny, I think I kin talk the town council inta lettin' me have a deputy. You kin rent a room over top of Della's Beanery fer ten dollars a month with meals thrown in."

"Well, I was planning to go up to Ellis and see what the city has to offer for a change."

"Sure, I understand. Rattlesnake Flats isn't much ta see. There's a lot more goin' on up in the big city."

By the time they got to the doctor's office, Jared was feeling tired. The bullet in his back seemed to burn like a hot coal.

The doctor's back was turned to them when they walked in. For a doctor, the person looked small, like a child, and was wrapping a little girl's wrist.

"Doc, this here is Clay Jared," the marshal said. "He's special, so treat him right."

Jared had been staring at the long hair and when he heard a voice he knew the doctor was a woman.

"Run along now, Milly!" the doctor said. She gave the girl a stick of hard candy and the little girl left.

The doctor turned around to look up. Jared's eye fastened on her face. It was pretty, so pretty that Jared couldn't stop staring. She noticed and smiled. For a while they stared at each other, seeming to enjoy the moment as if no one else were in the room.

The old marshal broke the spell.

"Jared, this is Doc Lauren Goodwin. She's the sawbones of Rattlesnake Flats. Doc, meet Clay Jared. He got winged in the back."

"Let's take a look, Mr. Jared," Lauren said.

Jared removed his jacket and vest, pulled his shirt up above his waist and turned his back to show her the wound. He felt her fingers on his back.

"The bandage is stuck to the wound. I'll have cut it off."

"Sure, Doc. Go ahead."

A moment later he felt the scissors cut the bandage. The loose ends fell away, but part of it stuck to the dried-up wound.

"I'll have to soak it, Mr. Jared."

"Alright, Doc," Jared replied. It seemed strange calling a woman a doctor.

"This may sting."

"Okay."

Jared smelled the pungent scent of medicinal alcohol, then an icy coldness on the wound. The coldness quickly began to turn to fire. He grunted in pain as he felt her dabbing away. It was as if she were using barbed wire.

"This may take a moment to soak in," Lauren said. Then, "What's so special about you, Mr. Jared?"

"Nothing," Jared replied, wincing in pain and inhaling deeply to keep from fainting.

"Don't be modest, Mr. Jared," Lauren said, almost mockingly. "The marshal here says you're special. Why is that?"

"Best ask the marshal, ma'am," Jared said haltingly, gasping for air.

"Alright, Marshal Nelson, why is Mr. Jared so special, sir?"

"Well, ma'am, he jest brought in the men what robbed the town bank, an' the money, too."

"Oh, really?"

"Yes, ma'am," the marshal said as if boasting.

"And were they alive, those bank robbers?"

"Ah, not hardly, ma'am. As a matter of fact, they was all dead as doornails," the marshal chuckled.

"I see," Lauren said dryly. "Mr. Jared is a bounty hunter, a killer of men, is he? Is that what you are, Mr. Jared, a killer of men?"

The words hit hard, and for a moment Jared wished he were someplace else. An uneasy calm followed during which no one spoke.

"Did you get your reward, your blood money, Mr. Jared?"

Jared remained silent.

"Now, Doc," the marshal said, "don't be so hard on the man. He did the town a great service."

"Of course he has, Aaron. He's done the killing for us, hasn't he? We should be grateful, shouldn't we? Our hands are clean."

Jared turned his head to smile at the doctor.

"I guess this means we can't be lovers."

The doctor gave him a cold look.

"Mr. Jared, will you please count to three, sir?"

"I can't count that high," Jared said, trying to cool the doctor down with a little humor. It didn't work. She still gave him that cold as steel look. "Alright. One and two and---"

Rip! The doctor yanked the bandage off the wound with a single jerk, stretching the flesh around the wound until it tore. Jared gasped and his knees almost buckled.

"Don't be a crybaby, Mr. Killer of Men," Lauren said. "A little thing like this shouldn't hurt you, should it?"

Jared sucked air like a fish out of water.

"Christ!" he gasped.

She reached over and picked up a deadly-looking probe from a tray of alcohol. "I don't approve of killing under any circumstances. My job is healing. Evidently yours is killing."

She swabbed his wound with alcohol again and again. The pain was intense enough to take his breath away.

"Hold still now, Mr. Jared. I'll have to pull the bullet out. This may hurt even more, so try to be brave, won't you?"

Before he could utter a word, he felt the probe go into the wound, hit the bullet, grab onto it and yank it out.

All Jared could do was grind his teeth and hiss like a snake.

"There, my brave friend," Lauren said. "All we have to do now it sew you up and you'll be good as new. I'll try to be gentle." There was an element of sadistic humor in her words.

The marshal brought a stool over for Jared to sit on.

"Thanks, Marshal," the cowboy managed to say.

The ten stitches felt like red-hot needles stabbing into his flesh. When it was done, Jared was sapped of energy and emotion. He sat on the stool hunched over.

"Jesus," he muttered.

Doctor Goodwin reached into a cabinet and found a pint bottle of whiskey. She poured some into a glass and handed it to Jared.

"Here, Mr. Jared, you've earned this."

Jared tossed it down in one pull.

"Another?" she asked. He nodded and she poured again.

He drank again and began to feel better.

The marshal chuckled. "She's a damn good sawbones, ain't she, Jared?" The cowboy nodded.

Lauren put some salve on the wound and wrapped it several times with gauze. Jared tucked his shirt back in, put on his vest and jacket then stood up.

"Thanks Doc. How much do I owe you?"

"It's on me, Mr. Jared," Lauren Goodwin said. She added with a hint of sarcasm, "You being special and all."

Jared put a hundred-dollar bank note on the table.

"Please take this," he said. "Buy some more of that stuff you tortured the hell outta me with."

His sarcasm hit home. She tilted her head a bit and shrugged.

"Alright, then," she replied. "It's for the next time you come in. Let's hope it isn't with a bullet in your heart. I'd hate to see that. Goodbye, sir."

Jared chuckled. She knew how to hit back.

He and the marshal left for the jail. Instead of mounting up, Jared went inside with him.

"About that deputy job, Marshal, I'd like to try it out."

The marshal chuckled. "She turned yer head good, didn't she, sonny? Well, don't git any ideas. Cole Zanuck is after her, an' he usually gits what he wants."

Jared shrugged. He wasn't interested in who Cole Zanuck was right then.

"I'll take my horse down to the stables for a feed and a rubdown. He's worn out. I'll leave him there for the night."

"Good. Then go up to Della's place, just past the bank. I'll meet you there after I talk to the town council about hiring you."

A half hour later Jared was eating at Della's place. A half hour after that, the marshal came in smiling. Della, a small pixie a few years younger than the lawman, greeted him with a hug and a kiss. The marshal blushed and told her to behave.

He turned to Jared. "All I gotta do is swear ya in, Jared."

Later Jared found himself standing in the jailhouse raising his right hand and taking the oath to become the new deputy of Rattlesnake Flats.

He took a room at Della's place. The next day he found himself going up and down the streets and alleys of Rattlesnake Flats scooping up horse and dog poop.

At that moment he regretted having ever met Doctor Lauren Goodwin.

3.

It didn't take cowboy Clay Jared long to learn that being a deputy was not the exciting and romantic job described in pulp magazines. Besides scooping up dog poop, he had to keep the main street and alleys of town clean of whiskey bottles, newspapers, or any other discarded refuse lying about. He was also responsible for handling disorderly people such as drunks, drifters and derelicts.

Another job was setting up the jury room in the Bar Z Saloon, which was owned by Cole Zanuck, a prominent and much respected citizen of Rattlesnake Flats. The trials, which were basically fines given out for drunken or disorderly conduct, were conducted by the bank manager Otis Jensen, who was the most educated person in town, having a degree in financing.

The real law hadn't gotten to Rattlesnake Flats as yet. The marshal was a town council appointed position and it set the salary at forty dollars a month, with no benefits added.

Jared learned that the governing body of Rattlesnake Flats was, in fact, the town council. It was comprised of newspaper owner Arthur Milner, who published the *Rattlesnake Flats Gazette*, a four-page, once a week periodical. The council also included Gil Baxter, owner of Baxter's Mercantile, the undertaker Uriah Freed, Otis Jensen, the bank manager, and Cole Zanuck, owner of the Bar Z Saloon.

As for the deputy position, it was open to the whims of the town council. A deputy might be called on to do almost anything, depending on the situation at hand.

Jared quickly learned that Cole Zanuck had his sights set on Lauren Goodwin. So far their relationship was still at the courting stage. They were often seen eating together in Della Lang's place.

When that reality started to sink in, Jared began to question his motives for taking the deputy job. He was a cowboy by trade and always would be. He was used to the wide open spaces, the fresh air and being close to nature. No, this had been a big mistake and he would correct it as soon as possible.

Jared was just about to hang up his badge and ride on when the marshal took him aside. "I got somethin' I want ya ta do, Jared."

"What?" Jared replied.

"Go down to Doc Goodwin's place. Leave yer horse here. You'll be driving her buckboard out to Miss Ella's place."

"Where's that?"

"The Doc will show ya. After you pick her up, stop at Gil Baxter's mercantile an' pick up some stuff. He'll have it already boxed up."

Jared wanted to ask more questions, but held off. He'd ask Doc Goodwin on the way out.

Lauren Goodwin was waiting in front of her place holding her doctor's bag. She was wearing a bonnet, blouse, skirt and boots. Her buckboard was at the rail, ready to go.

"Hi, Doc."

"Hello, Mr. Jared. How nice to see you again. How is your wound coming along?"

"Fine."

Lauren glanced at his deputy badge and smiled. Suddenly he felt exposed, found out.

As they got into the buckboard, she said, "I see you decided to change your lifestyle."

"This isn't permanent, ma'am," Jared said. "I thought I'd try it out for a while."

"Of course," Lauren said, then added, "Come see me tomorrow and I'll take a look at your wound."

"Sure."

Jared found it hard not to stare at her and she seemed to know it. Just sitting next to her in the buckboard bothered him.

Damn that marshal. He had planned it this way, the meddling old fart!

"Who's this Miss Ella?"

"Ella Morrison. She's the widow of the town's founder, Dave Morrison. They had a big farm once, outside of town, which is where we're going. There's nothing left to it now, though. She sold most of the land to the cattlemen."

"She must go back a long way. How old is she?"

"I don't know. I suspect she's in her seventies."

"And she lives out there by herself?"

"Yes."

"How does she do it?"

"She's living off her root cellar, chickens, pigs and her garden."

"How long can she last doing that?"

"Maybe six more months. A year."

Jared looked across the bench at Lauren. "What are you doing in a small place like this? You'd do better in the big city, wouldn't you?"

"It's a matter of ideals and choice," Lauren said. "Like you being a deputy. A town like this needs a doctor as well as a marshal. Anyway, I have rich parents in St. Louis. I can pack up and go back there any time I choose to."

"Well, it's very fine that you're here," Jared said.

"Thank you."

"What about Mr. Zanuck?"

"What about him?"

"You two are close, aren't you?"

"He's a fine man. And a good businessman, too."

"The rumor out there is he wants to marry you."

Lauren chuckled. "Is that the rumor out there?"

"Yup."

Jared had only seen Cole Zanuck from a distance and what he saw impressed him. The man was tall, dark and handsome and was always dressed in a suit, tie and Stetson. He didn't wear a gun, as far as Jared could tell.

"He doesn't wear a gun," Lauren said, as if reading his mind. "And that's what I like about Cole."

"You don't care for guns, do you?"

"No, I don't!" she said emphatically.

After that they didn't talk any more. The sun was warm, but there was an August breeze. White clouds moved west across a blue sky. They saw an eagle wheeling high up on the currents, a solitary hunter.

"Do you think it sees us?" Lauren asked.

"I'm sure it does. They don't miss much."

"This land is so beautiful," she said. "It's the real reason I came here. To be close to nature."

Jared nodded. At least they had that in common.

Miss Ella's place was about ten miles west of Rattlesnake Flats, just off the Colby to Atwood City coach road. The road ran through the Flats and on through fields of bluestem and wild rye where flocks of crows flitted about. As the buckboard passed them, they shot into the air like black diamonds sparkling in the sunlight.

Jared saw Miss Ella's place a mile ahead, a two-story frame structure with white clapboard siding and a root cellar beneath. As they rode closer they saw three horses tied to the fence.

"Looks like she's got company," Jared said.

"Looks that way."

Jared drove the buckboard through the open gate and tied up at the hitching post in front of the porch. As he and Lauren got down, two men came out of the house.

Jared quickly sized them up.

They were big men, filthy and scruffy looking, and wore ragged clothes that needed washing and mending. They could have been cowboys or just drifters. It was hard to tell, but they both wore guns.

Lauren approached the porch steps with her bag, staring up at them.

"What kin I do fer ya, ma'am?" the tallest one asked.

"I'm Doctor Goodwin. I've come to see Miss Ella."

"We'll, she ain't seein' nobody right now," the short one said. Something was wrong with his left eye. It stayed closed.

"May I ask who you are, sir?"

"Sure, ma'am. I'm her son," the short one replied.

"Yeah. Me, too, ma'am," the tall one added. He had a long scar along his left cheek.

"She doesn't have any sons."

"She does now," the short one chuckled. "Right, Bert?"

"She sure does, Matt!" the tall one replied.

Suddenly Lauren shouted, "Miss Ella! Are you alright?"

They heard Miss Ella start to yell back, but stopped. Her voice was suddenly muffled as if someone had put a hand over her mouth.

"They're hurting her!" Lauren said to Jared and started up the steps.

The two men drew their guns.

Lauren heard two rapid shots and then the sickening thud of a bullet as it slammed into the tall man's chest, knocking him flat on his back. The second bullet drilled a hole between the small man's eyes, snapping his head back on his neck and sending him dancing a crazy dance up against the wall of the house where he fell down in a heap.

A second later Jared was running up the porch steps past Lauren and into the house. He stopped in the hallway to look around, his gun at the ready.

"Don't come in here!" A gruff voice said from the living room. "I'll kill her!"

Jared put his Colt back in its holster.

"Let's talk," Jared said.

Lauren came up behind him.

"Stay here," Jared whispered to her. He walked into the living room.

A chubby, grizzly looking man stood behind the small, frail body of Miss Ella, using her for a shield. One hand was covering her mouth while the other held a knife to her throat. When the man saw Jared he grinned.

"Where's the bitch?"

"She's in the hall."

"Git her in here!"

"Tell me what you want," Jared said. He lowered his right hand slowly down by his holster. "What is it? Money? Food?"

"I already et," the man growled in a rusty voice. "I want yer gun an' yer money."

"Then what?"

"After I kill you, I'll take the bitch. She sounds young. Is she young?"

"Yes."

"Good. I likes 'em young," the man said. "Now hand over thet gun a yers. Bring it over here, handle first, or I'll cut the ol' lady's head off!"

Jared said. "Sure, but take it easy, fellah."

Jared looked at Miss Ella and nodded. She stared back at him, closed her eyes, then bit down on the man's hand. As he pulled away, screaming in pain, Miss Ella danced to one side. Jared drew and shot the outlaw in the chest three times, driving him across the room against the wall where he settled down into a sitting position.

The gunshots echoed loudly off the walls.

Lauren ran into the living room and straight to Miss Ella. The old lady had a defiant look on her face. She spat on the floor and wiped her mouth with her hand.

"How dare thet sidewinder put his greasy fingers in my mouth!" She spat again.

"Are you alright, Miss Ella?" Lauren asked.

"Oh, I guess I'm okay." She stared at Jared. "Who's this handsome young devil?"

"I'm Clay Jared, ma'am. Marshal Nelson's deputy."

"Well, you sure earned yer money taday, young man."

"I try, ma'am."

Jared reloaded his Colt as he walked over to the body. He grabbed it by the ankles, dragged it outside and dropped it next to the other two on the porch.

"Don't forget the supplies!" Lauren yelled out to him.

Jared went to the buckboard, picked up the box of food and carried it into the kitchen. Miss Ella stood at the stove making coffee. She was as spry as a spring colt, flitting around the kitchen, ninety pounds of pure energy.

"They had some nerve, bushwhacking me like that," Miss Ella complained. "Comin' in here like they did an' pushin' me around in my own house on my own land! They got jest what they had a-comin' ta them, tha sidewinders!"

She stopped to glance at Jared.

"When I talk ta thet town council, I'll see you get a raise, young man. How much are they payin' you?"

"Twenty a month," Jared replied.

"Well, you're worth twice that and I'll see thet you get it." She turned to Lauren. "Maybe you should stop messin' around with that carpetbagger Cole Zanuck an' put yer brand on Jared, here."

Lauren quickly changed the subject. "Miss Ella, you have to move into town. You can't live out here all alone like this. It's just too dangerous. After today, you see that now, don't you?"

The old lady shook her head as she poured the coffee.

"No, I can't do thet, honey. I'll die in town. My roots are here. An' my Davey is buried up behind the house by the big pine tree. I can't leave him all by his self. He's a-waitin' fer me. It won't be long afore we're together agin up in heaven. A kissin' and a-sparkin' like when we was young."

She smiled as her voice trailed off. Shaking the vision from her mind, Miss Ella got a wild-berry pie from the cupboard and cut two pieces.

"I hope ya like my wild-berry pie, Deputy Jared."

"If it tastes as good as it smells, I know I will."

Miss Ella sat down watching her visitors eat. When they were finished, Lauren helped the old lady put the box of staples away. Jared put the empty crate back in the buckboard.

Lauren stayed inside with Miss Ella while Jared tied the dead outlaws over their horses, then tied the reins of the horses to the back of the buckboard.

Miss Ella and Lauren came out on the porch. The old widow stood on her toes and gave Jared a big hug with a kiss on the cheek.

"God bless you, Clay Jared," she said. Her eyes were moist as she held back tears of gratitude.

"Are you sure you won't come to town with us, Miss Ella? You can put up at Della's place," Lauren asked.

The old matriarch shook her head.

"No. You two run along, now. I'll be fine. I like the peace and quiet here." Suddenly she glanced at the bodies of the three dead outlaws and laughed. "Well, it's peaceful here most of the time."

Lauren gave Miss Ella a hug and a kiss, then climbed into the buckboard next to Jared. Jared snapped the reins and they rode slowly out of the yard, waving at the tiny figure on the porch as they left.

4.

"Good God, sonny," the old marshal said. "If you keep a-drillin' these sidewinders we'll have ta build a new boneyard. Thet's six new graves in less than a month!"

Jared and Marshal Nelson were sitting in chairs on the jailhouse porch with their heels up on the railing. It was Friday afternoon and they sat there looking up and down Rattlesnake Flats' main street.

"It sure is quiet fer a Friday afternoon," the marshal observed. "In the old days, before the big winter kill, cowboys would come ta town by the dozens an' raise all kinds a hell. Herds were always a-comin' up the Western Trail, crossin' the Beaver River near here."

"I like it better like this," Jared chuckled.

They listened to the sounds of the town. A cat scowled and ran across the street, chased by a dog.

"Go arrest thet dog," the marshal chuckled. Jared laughed.

They heard loud voices arguing down at the Bar Z Saloon.

"I hope a fight don't break out down there," the marshal said.

"Yeah."

A middle-aged couple walked by holding hands. The lawmen nodded to them. They exchanged greetings.

Birds dropped down into the street, foraging for food, skittering around, chattering and taking flight again.

"How are you an' the Doc getting along?"

"We aren't."

"I guess you found out she hates guns an' killin', didn't ya?"

"Well, it was guns and killing that saved her and Miss Ella last week. I hope she sees that."

The marshal chuckled.

"Speakin' of Miss Ella, the town is puttin' on a shindig out at her place fer what they think is her seventy-fifth birthday."

"They must think a lot of her."

"They sure do. Miss Ella and her husband Davey made this town. Way back then, it was a stage stop between Colby and Atwood City, a place ta change horses and eat."

The marshal stopped a moment to collect his thoughts.

"Yep! Davey an' Ella Morrison got off thet stage one day an' it weren't long before they had a farmer's market goin'. When the cattle herds crossed the Beaver River nearby, they came looking ta buy fresh vegetables, fruits and home-brewed beers and such. Then Gil Baxter, who was a travelin' salesman, selling sundries from the back of a wagon, stopped an' stayed. One by one, others came an' planted roots, people like the blacksmith, Tom Sloan."

"Who named the town?"

The marshal scratched his chin and frowned.

"Hell, I never did figure thet out. I suppose it was Davey."

"Did you know him?"

"Oh, sure. He only died about five years back. Nice feller."

"So, the town grew?"

"Yep. There was ranches all around Davey's farm. An' they got along jest fine, too, because they needed what Davey grew. Ya couldn't live on jest beef an' nothin' else."

"When did Zanuck come in?"

"About three years ago Zanuck got off the stage and walked inta the saloon owned by Jim Derby. It was called the Bar D Saloon back then. By the end of the month, Zanuck owned it and re-named it the Bar Z."

"What happened to Derby?"

"The next day he jest rode off. Didn't say adios ta nobody."

Jared thought that was strange. "You knew Jim Derby well?"

"Oh, sure. He was on the town council."

"And he just rode off without a word?"

"Yep."

For a moment Jared let his words take root in the old marshal's mind. He could see by the look on his face that he knew there were unanswered questions concerning Jim Derby's sudden departure.

Finally, the marshal shuddered as if throwing off a chill. "About thet shindig out at Miss Ella's place," he said, "you an' me gotta be there."

"How come?"

"Jest ta keep things in order. Ta settle down any drunks or break up any fights over gals, which sometimes occur."

"Who's going to be there?"

"The whole town, I imagine. And what's left of the cowboys in the area. Wherever there's dancin' an' gals, you'll find cowboys."

"What about the bank? With everybody out of town, it's a sitting duck, isn't it?"

"Yeah," the marshal said. "I'll bring thet up at the town council meeting on Monday."

Monday came and the marshal attended the town council meeting at six in the evening, after the bank closed. Later, he walked back to the jailhouse and spoke to Jared.

"Zanuck said he'll have some men come down from Atwood City ta keep an eye on the bank," the marshal said.

"What kind of men?"

"Zanuck says it's a security company that specializes in guardin' banks, trains an' important big-wigs."

"That's real nice of him," Jared said.

"Yep. He's an upstanding citizen, alright."

On the day of the shindig, Jared and the marshal left town early in the afternoon. As they rode into the yard, Miss Ella came out to greet them with a smile and a hug.

She took Jared's arm and held it fast. "You have a good man here in Jared, Marshal. You'd best treat him right or I'll come after you." She invited them in for coffee.

"When are you moving into town, Miss Ella?" the marshal asked.

"Never. I ain't never movin' into town, Marshal, an' you darn well know it. An' you kin tell that to Doctor Goodwin, too."

Jared and the marshal finished their coffee and stood up to go.

"You two go over to the barn," Miss Ella said. "I'll come over after I take care of some chores here."

"Do ya need some help, Miss Ella?" the marshal asked.

"No, no. You two run along now."

Jared and the marshal walked over to the barn. "She sure is a stubborn cuss," the marshal muttered.

Men and women, all volunteers from town and from the nearby farms and ranches, were finishing the last touches. They had already set up benches along two walls.

Over to one side a few yards from the door was a long table filled with platters of smoked ham, baked ribs, roasted chickens and ducks. All this was cut and sliced for eating as is or in sandwiches. For the making of sandwiches there were platters of sliced bread.

On the dessert side were apple, peach and cherry pies and assorted cookies. Several bowls of punch completed the inventory.

On a separate table were two kegs of beer with cups and glasses. Also on this particular table were jars of pickled eggs and cucumbers for snacking. Everyone knew this table was donated by Cole Zanuck.

Three men with musical instruments sat in chairs on a platform in front of an open dance area. One had a violin, one a banjo and one a mouth harp. They seemed to be having a discussion of a humorous nature, as every so often they would burst out laughing.

Then there was the cake table, a small table with a large, double layer cake with white icing and the numbers 75 in large, blue letters on it.

It wasn't long before people from town and the surrounding area started arriving on horses, buckboards and carriages. Zanuck and Lauren came in his special two-person coach. She wore an elegant, strapless white silk dress that contrasted with his dark blue tweed suit, white shirt and black tie.

Jared noticed that she had changed her working boots for more delicate sequined slippers. He wondered how often she got to dress like this. She looked beautiful.

As they entered, Zanuck greeted the marshal warmly but ignored Jared. Lauren glanced at him, smiled and moved on without a word. He saluted her with a touch of his hat brim as she went by.

In a short time the yard was full and so was the barn. Oil lamps were lit and hoisted aloft on ropes attached to the barn rafters. Soon a man walked up beside the musicians. He had a short discussion with them and turned to face the crowd.

For a moment he stood there smiling, then began to clap and stomp his foot until the musicians started playing in harmony with his rhythm.

> *"Choose yer partner, form a ring,*
> *Figure eight, an' double L swing!*
> *First swing six an' then swing eight,*
> *Swing 'em like an' ol' barn gate!*
> *Ducks in tha river, goin' to tha ford,*
> *Coffee in a little pot, sugar in a gourd!"*

People came to the floor and the dancing started.

Jared and the marshal stood by the door watching as newcomers arrived. The men hung their guns up on wall pegs next to the entrance and went to join the fun.

Jared set his eyes on Cole Zanuck and Lauren Goodwin as they danced. After a set of group dances, the musicians changed the pace and played waltzes. Zanuck held Lauren close. They looked good dancing together. The marshal noticed it, too.

"They sure make a mighty fine couple," he chuckled, staring at Jared to see the effect of his words.

Jared shrugged and said nothing.

Lauren and Zanuck were on their second waltz when a young cowboy, one who'd had a little too much to drink, swaggered up and tapped Zanuck on the back. Zanuck gave him a patronizing glare and kept on dancing. The cowboy, not wanting to look foolish to his friends, kept at it, following Zanuck and Lauren around the floor, tapping him on the shoulder, wanting to dance with Lauren.

"Oh, oh! This ain't good," the marshal said. "This ain't good at all!"

Jared watched, fascinated. "Should we do something?" he asked.

"It ain't no problem yet," the marshal said. "The cowboy probably knows the Doc. She's treated most all of 'em one time or another."

"Zanuck isn't too happy," Jared said.

Suddenly Zanuck turned and shoved the cowboy as hard as he could. The young man went reeling backwards against several other dancers, then tripped and fell to the floor. Everyone stopped dancing and backed away.

"You shouldn't a-done thet, mister!" the cowboy yelled.

He came fast up from the flooring and swung at Zanuck, connecting with a wild blow that sent the older man staggering backwards and down on his knees. Just as the cowboy moved in to hit him again, Zanuck pulled a derringer from his inside coat pocket and shot him in the chest.

The cowboy stopped in his tracks, a dazed look on his face. He put a hand to his chest and stared dull-eyed at the blood on it.

"I jest wanted a dance with Miss Lauren," he said and sank slowly to the floor. A young girl let out a high-pitched scream and dropped down beside him, cradling him in her arms,

"We was gonna be married," she screamed at Zanuck.

For a moment Zanuck looked scared, uncertain, unsure. His swaggering self-confidence was gone.

"It was self-defense!" he yelled, looking around for support. He found none.

Lauren ran to the boy's side and opened his shirt to look at the wound. Zanuck's bullet had gone into his heart. In her rush to help, she got some blood on one hand. She stared at it for a moment then unconsciously wiped it on her white dress. Everyone stared at the red stain it made.

Zanuck backed away, glaring at the crowd. "It was self-defense, I tell you!"

The crowd seemed to have other ideas. Friends of the cowboy began to close in on Zanuck, forming a circle around him. Several started to reach out and grab him.

"Now it's a problem," the marshal shouted. He shoved his way through the crowd and finally got beside Zanuck. "Back off, folks! Let the law take care of this!"

"Hang that city slicker!" someone yelled.

Shouts of anger came from the crowd. "He shot young Bill over a damn dance! It ain't right!"

The marshal took the derringer from Zanuck and tucked it in his belt. Jared looked around for Lauren and saw she was standing next to Zanuck looking frightened.

Suddenly the marshal took out his gun and waved it above his head. The crowd froze in place.

"He's my prisoner!" the marshal yelled. "I'm a-takin' him in ta the jailhouse! Now, all of you back away an' give me some room before I git real mad an' arrest all a ya!"

This seemed to satisfy the crowd for the moment. The marshal knew he had to work fast before some rabble-rouser started trouble. At any moment they would demand a lynching instead of a trial, and he'd be helpless to prevent that. Court law, to them, was too slow and unpredictable. They wanted frontier justice, justice of the people and by the rope.

"You have to protect me, Marshal!" Zanuck yelled. He was almost shaking with fear.

"I'm takin' you in, Zanuck," the marshal yelled so the crowd could hear, "an arrestin' ya fer murder!" He pointed his gun at Zanuck, grabbed his arm and dragged him through the crowd towards the door. One old man got a good swing and punched Zanuck on the back, knocking the air out of his lungs.

The marshal saw Jared a few feet behind.

"Jared," he shouted, "find Miss Lauren! Bring her in Zanuck's carriage!" Jared nodded that he understood.

The marshal and his prisoner were surrounded all the way out into the yard. He got on his mount and waved his gun barrel at Zanuck.

"Git on Jared's horse!"

Zanuck climbed on Jared's horse and they rode out for town at a fast gait. Curses and rocks followed them until they were out of sight.

People began to mount up and leave. The party was over.

Jared looked around for Lauren. When he couldn't find her, he went back inside. She was with the young girl who stood crying over the dead cowboy, holding her hand, trying to comfort her. A few people stood nearby. The women cried. The men shook their heads in anger and frustration.

"In the old days, we'd a-hanged thet sidewinder!" one remarked. The others nodded.

Jared took off his hat and stood with his head bowed. Lauren finally saw him and walked over.

"Where's Cole? Is he safe?"

"The marshal took him to town. He's riding my horse. I'll take you back in Zanuck's carriage."

"Alright," Lauren said. She looked confused.

"Did you know him?" Jared asked.

"The young man? Yes. Bill Elroy. I set his broken arm last year. He just turned nineteen," she said as if her mind was fogged and she was still trying to figure out what had happened.

"Come on," Jared said. "You can't do anything now."

Miss Ella came walking into the barn. She saw the dead cowboy, put her hand to her mouth and gasped. She rushed over to the girl, said some comforting words and hugged her. Finally, she came over to Lauren and Jared.

"They told me what happened," she said in a voice heavy with concern. "How sad. Are you alright, Doc?"

"No, not really," Lauren sighed. "I still can't believe what just happened. It was so quick. One minute I was dancing a lovely waltz and then the world exploded."

"Come up to the house," Miss Ella said. "We'll have coffee."

"Thank you, but I should be going, Miss Ella."

Miss Ella looked at Jared. "Thet Zanuck. I never liked thet man. There's something about him thet smells rotten."

Before Jared could answer, the girl came up to him. "Is he gonna git away with murderin' my Billy?" she asked.

50

"He'll stand trial," Jared replied. "An honest jury will find him guilty, I'm sure."

"What if they don't? What then?"

"Then it's in God's hands, ma'am," was all that Jared could think of saying.

He and Lauren left for town.

5.

The Rattlesnake Flats town council was not too happy with their favorite son in jail. Mayor Otis Jensen, Arthur Milner, Gil Baxter and Uriah Freed all voted to have him released on his own recognizance. Marshal Nelson argued that he couldn't be responsible for Zanuck's safety as there were certain people in the area who wanted to see him dancing from a rope.

Zanuck found an agreeable solution by hiring two private bodyguards from the Atwood City Security Company. He also hired the Atwood City law firm of Davis, Mapes and Slopes to defend him in court. As for the upcoming trial, Zanuck's law firm had the venue changed from Rattlesnake Flats to Atwood City. The date was yet to be determined.

The situation split the community into two groups, the town's elite against the area's working classes, which were mostly cowboys, ranchers, farmers and the painted ladies who hung around the Bar Z Saloon. The newspaper ran an editorial asking for calm on both sides of the issue.

Tensions were high and the marshal and his deputy were caught square in the middle. Lauren remained silent and brooding. Jared could see her inner turmoil. Zanuck was a big part of her life.

When Jared went to have the doctor look at his wound, she seemed cold and distant. He sensed that she was conflicted about her relationship with Zanuck.

Deep down inside, Jared thought, she must know that Zanuck had committed cold blooded murder. The cowboy was unarmed and Zanuck was armed. He was a coward and had violated the code by shooting an unarmed man. Everyone in the barn had seen him do it, including her.

After she put a new dressing on the wound, he offered to pay her. "How much, Doc?"

"Nothing," she said coldly.

He put three double eagles on the table and started to leave.

"Jared, wait!" Her voice sounded urgent. He stopped and turned towards her. She stared at him for a moment and looked away. "Nothing," she said.

A few days later Jared sat in the jail watching the marshal go over some wanted circulars that had been dropped off by the mail stage. They came from Atwood City on a regular basis.

"Anything new, Marshal?"

"Yep, plenty new. I recognize a lot of these here names."

"Friends of yours?" Jared chuckled.

The marshal got a serious look on his face. "Some were, yes. Most of 'em were hardworking cowboys. When thet big freeze killed off the herds, it left them without a job, so some of 'em turned ta robbin' trains an' banks an' such."

"I didn't."

"No, an' good fer you, sonny. You're one of the lucky ones. Or maybe you were smarter, I don't rightly know."

Jared felt chastised, so he shut up.

"Take this one," the marshal said, handing Jared a circular of an outlaw called Bax Carter. There was a description, but no drawing.

"You know him?"

The marshal nodded.

"Yep, he was ramrod of the Lazy R, over by Colby City, fer nigh on ten years. It was a big spread. Carter had maybe twenty cowpokes under him a-ridin' fer the brand. But thet big freeze came an' the Lazy R lost ninety percent of its beeves. Ol' man Reynolds, he cut all but five cowboys loose, includin' Bax, the ramrod. What a dirty deal thet was fer Carter."

"And now he's riding the outlaw trail."

"Yep. Ol' Bax is on the bad side of the law, now."

"How did you two meet?"

"The Lazy R used ta run their herds up north across the Beaver River near here. The Doc has treated most of the Lazy R boys for one ailment or another. They all liked her. Bax would bring the boys in ta git fixed up an' they'd end up in the Bar Z gittin' drunk. Of course it was the Bar D then, being owned by Jim Derby."

"Not to change the subject, boss," Jared said, "but it's sticking in my craw."

"What's stickin' in yer craw?"

"About Derby just sneaking off and never telling anyone where he was headed."

"Well, thet's how it happened, sonny."

"Maybe it did and maybe it didn't."

"If ya know somethin' I don't know, jest spit it out. Don't be bashful."

"Nope. It's just a feeling I have is all."

"Well, I wouldn't go around makin' claims I couldn't back up if I was you.

"I don't intend to, old man."

"Don't call me ol' man, sonny!"

"Don't call me sonny, old man!"

There was a short, tight silence, then both men broke out laughing.

Jared took out his makings and built a cigarette. He handed the pouch to the marshal. In a few moments they sat back, relaxed and smoked.

"Yeah," the marshal said. "It's plumb sad what thet freeze did. It jest about destroyed the cattle business."

"I got a feeling it's far from down and out," Jared said. "It'll come back with better breeds of stock. The ranchers are smarter now."

"I hope yer right," the marshal said.

Jared was about to say he was right when a man with a little girl came in.

"Hi, Jake," the marshal said. "Need somethin'?"

"The Doc," Jake said. "It's been two days now. She was supposed ta see my little girl."

"Two days, ya say?"

"Yep! Two days."

The marshal glanced at Jared with a worried look on his face. He told the man, "Alright, Jake, I'll look into it."

After the man and the girl left, the marshal stood up, stretched and walked out onto the porch. He flicked the cigarette butt into the street. Jared come out beside him.

"Let's go, Deputy," the marshal said. "We got a missin' person on our hands."

He stepped into the street and started across it in a hurry. Jared caught up with him.

"Where we headed?"

"Over to her office."

"The man said she ain't there."

"I heard what he said. I ain't deaf."

In a few minutes they were browsing around in Lauren Goodwin's office.

"Looks like she took her bag and stuff," the marshal noted.

"Her buckboard is gone, too."

"I'm guessin' she's out at Miss Ella's place?"

"For two days?"

The marshal shrugged. "I'll ride out there."

"I'll go with you."

They mounted and rode west out of town on the ten-mile stretch to Miss Ella's farm, pushing their mounts at a fast gait all the way. Both men and the horses were exhausted when they rode into the yard. Miss Ella came out on the porch holding a cup of coffee.

"What's the big rush, Marshal?"

"We're a-lookin' fer the Doc!"

"Somebody hurt in town?"

"It ain't thet. She's been a-missin' fer two days now. You ain't seen her, have ya?"

"No. She ain't been here, Marshal."

"Damn!"

"Come in fer coffee and pie."

"No, but we'd like ta water an' feed the horses."

"There's a water trough and plenty of oats in the barn," Miss Ella said.

"Thank ya."

Soon they were back on the road racing for town. When they got there, they went to see Gil Baxter at the mercantile.

"The Doc's gone. Have you seen her lately, Gil?"

"Two days ago, Marshal. She came in here and bought some food. Mostly cans of beans and peaches. And a smoked ham and some flour. I figured she was taking it out to Miss Ella's place."

They didn't say anything and left.

"What's next?" Jared asked.

The marshal sighed and scratched his chin. He seemed stumped. "I don't rightly know."

"Let's try Tom Sloan."

"The blacksmith? Yeah, might as well."

They rode down to the end of town to the blacksmith's shack. Sloan stopped working and came out to meet them.

"Yeah, as a matter of fact, I did see her leaving town. There was a cowboy with her. He was on a horse an' she was driving her buckboard," Sloan said. "Yep. Two days ago."

"What kind of horse was he riding?" Jared asked.

"A mustang, I think. Chestnut."

"He wasn't a cowboy," the marshal said. "Cowboys don't ride mustangs. Outlaws do."

"Which way you figure they're headed?" Jared asked.

"Since they headed north, my guess is they're headed in the direction of Beaver Creek," Sloan replied.

Jared and the marshal walked back to the jail to figure it out. "What the heck is she up to?" the marshal wondered.

They sat there in a funk, with worried looks on their faces, not knowing what to do next.

"Why would she take her bag, buy a mess a food and ride off with an outlaw?" Jared mused out loud.

The marshal gave that some thought for a moment then snapped his fingers. "Bax Carter!"

"What?"

"Bax Carter an' his boys! I bet a posse's got him and his boys holed up somewhere near Beaver Creek. An' he sent ta her fer help. He must be in real bad shape ta do thet."

"Christ!" Jared said, looking worried.

"You good at tracking, Jared?" the marshal asked.

"I did some. You?"

"Yeah. Plenty, when I was with the Rangers."

"Why do you ask, Marshal?"

"Why? Because the Doc is with the Bax Carter gang, is why, ya idgit! An' we gotta track her down!"

6.

Cole Zanuck came into the jailhouse with his two bodyguards. He ignored Jared and went straight at the marshal.

"Shouldn't you be looking for Miss Goodwin, Marshal?"

The bodyguards were dressed in tight fitting leather clothing, from their hats all the way down to their fancy black boots. They looked Jared over, with a smirk on their faces as if daring him to brace them.

Jared smiled.

"I hear you're pretty fast on the draw, Deputy," the tall, slim one said to Jared.

Jared shrugged. "There are a few people who think so."

"Maybe we'll get a chance to see how fast you are," the short one said.

"Maybe," Jared said calmly.

The marshal got up from his desk and faced Zanuck.

"We're jest leaving, Mr. Zanuck," the marshal said. "Would you an' yer men like ta come along?"

That set Zanuck back on his heels. For a moment he fumbled for an answer. He finally came up with, "It's not my job, Marshal. It's what the town pays you for. So I suggest you two get going."

The marshal walked slowly towards the door. Jared got up and brushed past the two gunnies, following the marshal out to the street. They mounted up, leaving Zanuck and his men looking on.

As they rode away, Jared said loudly, "He's sure a bossy asshole, ain't he?"

Zanuck had heard every word. He turned to the tall gunny and muttered angrily, "I want him dead!"

The tall one nodded. "Consider it done, Mr. Zanuck."

Jared and the marshal rode past the stables and north onto the road to Colby City.

"Where we headed?" Jared asked.

"There's an old line shack ten miles northeast of here. It used ta belong to the Box N spread when they was in business," the marshal said.

"You think that's where Carter is holed up?"

The marshal was looking down at the buckboard tracks. "I don't rightly know, but her tracks are headed in thet general direction. We'll sure find out soon enough."

They rode spread out on the road as it cut through a field of bluestem and gray sage. It led up a rise and then down into a shallow gully, eventually coming out into another field.

It was a clear, warm day and the sky was piled high with cotton clouds. High above, eagles swam the currents like gliding ships. A stagecoach came in their direction. They moved to one side. The passengers waved at them and yelled a greeting as it rattled and jolted past. The driver and the shotgun nodded. It left a trail of dust floating behind.

"Thet's the five-thirty fer Rattlesnake Flats," the marshal said.

They finally stopped at a stream and dismounted. As the horses drank, they took a pull from their canteens. Suddenly, Jared looked at the marshal. "Did you hear that?"

"No, what?"

"Listen!"

The marshal tilted his head. Finally, he nodded. "Gunfire?"

Jared nodded. "Gunfire!"

They mounted up and urged the horses into a run, following the dull, thundering sounds of gunfire. It led them to turn off the road into a stand of silver aspens. At its far end they stopped.

Down below, a hundred yards away, a group of about fifteen men lay spread out behind a berm, pouring lead into an old, weathered line shack. Jared could hear the bullets smash into the warped, dry wood. Splinters flew into the air like water spray. One man, the leader, ran back and forth shouting directions to the shooters. Their horses stood grounded in a pine stand behind them.

No return fire came back at them from the shack, but four horses and a buckboard were seen tied to some pine trees near it.

"Damn it! Thet's the Doc's buckboard," the marshal growled. "Let's git down there, Jared!"

They rode fast across the distance and came up behind the posse. Jared was out of his saddle before his mount came to a grinding stop, sending dirt flying everywhere. The marshal was at his side.

"Stop firing, you assholes!" he screamed. "There's a woman in there!"

They all stopped shooting to stare at the intruders.

A young man with a marshal's badge ran up to them. He was spitting mad.

"Who the hell are you two?" he yelled. When he saw their badges he cooled down some. "Oh. Well, we don't need any help here, fellahs."

"You from Colby City?" Marshal Nelson asked.

"That's right. What about it?"

"I'm Marshal Nelson from Rattlesnake Flats an' this is Clay Jared, my deputy. There's a woman in thet line shack. I'm responsible fer her safety."

The young lawman identified himself. "I'm Marshal James. You say a woman is in there? Who the hell is she and what the hell is she doing with Bax Carter and his bunch of bank robbers?"

"She's a doctor an' she's probably patchin' up the wounded," the marshal said.

The marshal from Colby City chuckled. "What the hell for? They're all either gonna die or hang!"

"You dumb sonofabitch," Jared growled. "Tell your men to stop shooting or I'll plug yer ass here and now!"

"An' if he don't, I will," Marshal Nelson growled, dropping his hand down by his Colt.

The young lawman looked a bit spooked. He glanced over at the shack for a moment then back at the marshal. "Okay. I'll give you a half hour to get her out of there." He shouted at his men. "Hold your fire, men! Marshal Nelson and his deputy are going in!"

The old marshal walked to the top of the berm and stopped. "Doc! It's me and Jared."

A rusty voice answered, "Is thet you Nelson, you old fart?"

"Yep, it's me, Bax, you ol' sidewinder! Kin we come in?"

"Yeah. Come an' git the Doc. I don't want her hurt!"

Jared and the marshal raised their hands and walked up to the splintered shack door. It opened and, as they went in, it closed behind them.

Jared saw Lauren Goodwin kneeling beside a grizzly looking old outlaw. It appeared he had three bullet wounds, one in the left side, one in the left arm and one in the right thigh.

She had a slight wound on her left shoulder.

Nearby, three young cowboys crouched down, staring at Jared and the marshal. They wore bandages where they had been shot in their arms and sides. All of them were in bad shape. Their faces were pale and they looked afraid, knowing this could only end one way.

"I'm a-dyin', Nelson," Bax Carter said.

"You shoulda stayed legal, Bax," the marshal said. "You was a damn good cowboy."

Carter coughed. "We was all cowboys once, wasn't we boys?"

They others nodded.

"You shoulda stuck ta ridin' fer the brand, old friend," the marshal said sadly. "You were never cut out fer this line a work, Bax."

"I reckon not. I kin see thet now," Carter said haltingly. "Thet fine lookin' fellah with ya, Marshal," Bax Carter said,

"I kin see he was a cowboy once. It's in his face an' eyes. He can't hide it, no sir, he can't hide it."

Blood bubbled up from the corner of Carter's mouth.

Lauren began to cry. The old outlaw stared up at her with half closed eyes.

"You been a real friend, Miss Lauren," Bax Carter said. "Thanks fer all yer help, ma'am. If I was younger, I'd come ta courtin' ya. I surely would."

Bax Carter closed his eyes with a deep sigh. Lauren looked up at Jared and the marshal. "Won't this senseless killing ever stop? It has to stop! Somebody must stop it!"

One of the wounded cowboys motioned to Lauren Goodwin. He hardly looked twenty years old. "Thank ya fer fixin' me up, ma'am, but ya gotta go now. You'll only die here." He looked up at Jared. "Please take her away, won't ya?"

Jared nodded and walked over to Lauren and lifted her up on her feet. "Get her bag, Marshal."

He picked Lauren up in his arms, walked to the door and yelled, "Hey, out there! We're coming out!"

He went outside. The marshal followed close behind.

"I'll git the buckboard," the marshal said.

Jared waited as the marshal led the buckboard horse over to him and Lauren. She was crying hard now. The men in the posse stared, confused, as Jared lifted her up on the bench and sat beside her.

After the marshal got his and Jared's horses and tied them to the rear of the buckboard, he climbed up beside Jared and Lauren. The young marshal came over. He stared at Lauren.

"I'm sorry, ma'am. I didn't know you were in there."

Lauren gave him a withering glare, but said nothing.

"Let's go," Jared said.

The marshal snapped the reins and the buckboard moved across the open area toward the trees.

"Oh, God! Oh, God! They're all going to die!" Lauren sobbed. She grabbed Jared's arm and buried her face against his shoulder. He could feel the hot wetness of her tears.

They were halfway to the trees when the shooting started again.

7.

A week later, the marshal and Jared sat in chairs on the jail porch with their heels up on the railing.

Jared reached under his vest into his shirt pocket and pulled out his tobacco pouch. He peeled a paper off, rolled a cigarette and handed the pouch to the marshal. In a few moments they were both leaning back and smoking.

"She's still takin' it bad," the marshal said.

"Yeah," Jared replied. "It's hit her hard."

"She's got a code, I guess."

"I hear all doctors take an oath of some kind."

The marshal nodded. "It's a-killin' her, Jared. She was tryin' ta save them and it's a-killin' her thet she couldn't."

"I think she finally got a good taste of the law out here and didn't like it one bit."

"Yeah, she came all the way out here ta save people an' all she sees is dyin' an' killin'."

They were quiet for a while, taking in the sounds of the town. A dog barked and it was a comforting sound. A man and a woman in a buckboard rode by them, and that was good to see because it was normal. The town seemed peaceful and orderly.

Yet, beneath it all was a lingering danger, ready to jump out and have its way. Nothing could stop it. It was as if someone or something was making it happen for their own pleasure.

Sometimes Jared felt the undercurrent. He waited for the explosion to happen, knowing that it could erupt like a volcano at any second. All he knew was that he had to stay alert, stay ready for it when it came.

"She'll be taking the staples out ta Miss Ella's place tomorrow. You should go with her."

"I went last time."

"My back is a-botherin' me. You gotta go."

Jared didn't believe the excuse about the back hurting. It didn't matter. He hadn't seen Lauren in a week and he was anxious to see her again. "Alright, I'll go then," he mumbled.

The marshal chuckled. "Yer not foolin' me, Jared. Yer dyin' ta see her."

The next day Jared and Lauren rode out of town for Miss Ella's place in Lauren's buckboard, leaving his horse down at the stable.

"How you doing, Doc?"

"Much better. I've managed to put it out of my mind."

Jared chuckled. "No, you haven't."

"What?" she asked.

"I said, no, you haven't. It ain't that easy. It'll take time. A long time."

She started to weep quietly. He glanced at her, watching her choke back her tears. She stared back at him. "Those three young boys. They had mothers and sweethearts and now they're all dead. They told me their names and I can't even remember them. Oh, God!"

He waited a moment for her to settle down. "That's how it is out here, Doc," Jared said. "You choose what trail to ride. Some trails lead to a posse hunting you down, and some trails don't."

"Have you ever thought of being an outlaw, Jared?" she asked, looking into his eyes.

"Thought about it? Heck, I came close to doing it."

"But, you didn't?"

"No, I didn't," Jared said. "Did you know that Marshal Nelson rode the outlaw trail when he was young?"

"He did? Really?"

"Yep. He spent five years in prison and after that went straight. He rode for the brand and later was a Texas Ranger. Outlaws make great lawmen. Marshal Nelson is one of the best I've ever met."

As they came around a bend in the road Jared brought the buckboard to a gentle stop.

"What's wrong?" Lauren asked.

Jared pointed to some bushes on the far edge of a field to their right. Lauren looked. At first she saw nothing, then saw a doe and her little fawn. The mother looked up at them as if sensing their gaze. Her ears turned, but she didn't move.

"They're so beautiful," Lauren whispered, smiling.

They sat looking at the mother and baby until they turned and ran off across the field into a stand of pine trees. Jared snapped the reins and they moved on again.

"They looked so sweet and innocent," Lauren said.

"They taste good, too," Jared said, chuckling.

She doubled her fist and hit him playfully on the shoulder. "That's not nice to say." She seemed a bit cheered up.

They soon rode into Miss Ella's yard and tied up at the porch rail. They sat there a moment looking around. "She might be back in the kitchen," Lauren said. "We might as well go in."

They dismounted. Jared got the crate of staples from the back of the buckboard, followed her into the kitchen and set it on the table. No one was there.

"She might be upstairs cleaning," Lauren said. "I'll look."

She walked out into the hallway and up to the second floor. Jared waited. She finally came down.

"She's not in the house," Lauren said. "She could be in the barn."

"She would have seen us come in from there," Jared said.

Lauren looked very worried. "Come on! She might have fallen and hurt herself!"

They rushed from the house, across the yard and into the big red barn. They rummaged around behind things for half an hour. As they started to leave, Lauren stopped a moment to look down.

There was a dark spot, a stain on the plank floor. It was the place where Zanuck had shot the young cowboy. Someone hadn't gotten it fully out. It lay like a reminder of the murder. Lauren shivered and they went out into the yard.

They stood there trying to figure out where Miss Ella was. "Maybe she went visiting someone," Jared said.

"Something's not right," Lauren said. "Look over there." She pointed to where some chicken and pigs were running loose. Every once in a while a pig would charge a chicken.

"They haven't been fed for a while," Jared said. "When pigs are hungry, they'll go after anything."

Suddenly they heard a dog bark and growl. "Does she have a dog?" Jared asked.

"No, but there's a stray that comes around sometimes. She tried to make a pet of it. But it doesn't stay long."

"What kind?"

"An old bloodhound. It was somebody's hunting dog, I suppose. Now it's wild."

"Yeah, dogs can do that out here. You have to keep an eye on them."

The dog growled again. "It's up behind the house," Jared said.

"That's where her husband is buried," Lauren replied.

The same thought struck them both, and they rushed around the house and up the slope.

That was when they saw Miss Ella.

She was sitting on the ground with her back against her husband Davey's headstone. Her thin arms hung by her side and she held a small bunch of wilted wildflowers in one hand. She looked very peaceful siting there with a smile on her lips, her eyes closed as if she were deep in thought. She had on a blue and white cotton polka-dot dress and looked very pretty with a red bow in her silver hair, looking as if she were just going on a date.

An old, mangy, flea-bitten hound dog stood at her feet. He was hunched forward in the attack position, snapping at two pigs who were trying to get at Miss Ella.

The old mutt looked about ready to fall over from hunger. When it saw Lauren and Jared, it ran off into the woods above the grave. Jared picked up a fallen branch and went at the pigs, chasing them off.

Lauren knelt down and took one of Miss Ella's frail hands in her own. It was cold. Jared came over.

"How long?"

"A day, at most," Lauren said. "If only I'd come sooner."

"You can't change things. It happened this way because it was meant to happen this way."

Lauren turned on him with an angry glare. It was so intense and fierce and powerful it shocked him.

"You and your cowboy stoicism! You think you know so damn much about life and death, don't you? Well, you don't! I've seen more death than you can ever imagine, you simple-minded man! I've brought people into this world and

I've watched them leave this world! So don't preach to me about life and death, cowboy!"

She stood up and faced him. He had felt the full force of the inner strength he always knew was there.

He backed off a little to give her more room, waiting for the next blast. He had earned it, deserved it, but it didn't come. Instead, she came into his arms, put her head on his chest and cried hard. Her body shook and she moaned sorrowfully. "I'm afraid, Jared. Please hold me."

He wrapped her in his arms and they stood swaying. The old hound dog howled mournfully back in the woods. "Listen, Doc," Jared said. "You're the bravest person I ever met. You're a real cowboy and I'd ride through the gates of hell with you if you ask me to."

His words of praise stopped her shaking. She looked up at him. "Do you mean that Jared, or is that just more talk?"

"I'm telling it true, Doc."

"It's our fault, all of us in town," Lauren said, sighing. "We should never have left her alone. I told them. They didn't listen. They were too busy with their own lives, I guess. The marshal cared more about her than the rest."

"We'll take her to town," Jared said.

"Alright."

It took a while. There were things to do.

Lauren got a sheet and blanket from the bedroom. Jared wrapped Miss Ella's body in them and placed her in the back of the buckboard along with the crate of staples. They tried, but had little success in, rounding up the pigs and chickens, so they just closed the house and barn doors and headed back to Rattlesnake Flats.

As they rode into town, word quickly spread.

Miss Ella is gone.

God bless Miss Ella.

8.

"How long did the Doc say she was dead?" the marshal asked.

Jared replied, "A day or two at most."

"What was she doin' out there in back? Hangin' out the wash?" the marshal asked.

"No, she was putting flowers on her husband's grave. She was all dressed up, too, like she was a young girl going on a date or something."

"It hit the Doc pretty hard, I imagine."

"It sure did. She cried like a baby."

They were sitting in their usual spot on the jail porch with their heels up on the railing. It was a little before the supper hour.

"I got a feeling about this," the marshal said.

"How so?"

Before answering, the marshal took time to roll a cigarette and light it. After taking a drag, he spoke.

"Now thet Miss Ella is gone, this town ain't gonna be the same no more. It'll change."

"In what way?"

"Well, she was sort of the backbone of this town. People respected her an' behaved like she was a school marm a-watchin' the kids. When they got too rowdy, she'd crack their knuckles good and they'd settle down an' behave. You know what I mean, Jared."

"Yeah, I guess I do."

"Yep, this town is gonna change. It's jest a feelin' I got. Like when yer joint hurts and ya know it's gonna rain. Ya know what I'm a-sayin', Jared."

Jared chuckled. "Ah, not really. When my joints hurt it's because I've been riding too long or working too hard."

Arthur Milner, the *Gazette* owner and publisher, came down the street and stopped.

"Hi, Deputy," Milner said to Jared in a friendly voice, nodding.

"Good evening, sir," Jared replied. "How's it going?"

"Just fine, Deputy," the newspaperman said. He looked at the marshal. "The council is going to meet at seven this evening, Marshal Nelson. You'd best come."

"I'll be there, Mr. Milner," the marshal said.

"Good. I'll tell them you're coming, then."

"I'll bring Jared here along."

A look of uncertainty came over Mr. Milner's face. "Ah, well, maybe not this time, Marshal. No offense meant, Deputy."

"None taken, sir," Jared said. "I've no need to be there. I'll just sit here and guard the town while you big-wigs chew the fat."

Mr. Milner chuckled. "Well said, young man, well said."

He looked at Jared for a moment as if studying his features. Finally, he nodded and went back up the street to his newspaper.

"Somethin' is a-bothering him," the marshal said. "Well, I'll find out this evenin'."

"He's a fine newspaperman," Jared said. He was a fan of the *Gazette* and read it every Friday when it came out.

The marshal chuckled. "His wife does most of the writin'. He's more or less the editor, is all."

Around seven that evening the marshal left for the council meeting. Jared sat on the jail porch for a while then walked up the street to Della's Beanery for a bowl of stew, pie and coffee. After that he went up to his room to wash up. He was in one of four rooms that Della rented out on the second floor.

It was almost sundown when Jared arrived at the jailhouse to find the marshal sitting at his desk. The marshal looked like he'd swallowed a lemon.

"What's wrong?" Jared said as he sat alongside the desk.

"Damn it," the marshal said, "I hate ta tell ya this, Jared, but I gotta let you go."

For a moment Jared was speechless. When it settled fully in, he nodded and said, "Okay. Sure."

"It wasn't my say. Thet sonofabitch Zanuck threatened to resign from the council and close up his business unless they cut you loose."

"It's okay, you don't have to explain."

"I managed ta git them ta let you stay until the end of the month."

Jared sat back and rolled a cigarette.

"When is Zanuck going up to Atwood City for his trial?"

"Tomorrow," the marshal said. "He's takin' the Doc with him. He says she needs a rest. They'll be back by the end of the month."

"That gives me about two weeks, then," Jared said.

"Two weeks fer what?"

"To find out what happened to Jim Derby, the original owner of the Bar Z Saloon."

The marshal chuckled.

"What the heck's wrong with you, Jared? I told you what happened to Jim Derby. He sold out to Zanuck an' left town. Did you forgit it already?"

"No, I didn't forget."

"What, then? What's eatin' at ya, boy?"

"The way it happened is what's eating at me. It doesn't seem right. Something is missing."

The marshal shook his head. "Well, good luck there, Jared. I'm afraid you'll be a-wastin' yer time. There ain't nothin' missing."

"I think there is."

"Yeah? Then tell me what it is."

"I can't put my finger on it just yet."

"You know what I think, Jared?"

"No, what?"

"I think yer mad as a wet hen at Zanuck over the Doc, an' yer lookin' fer a way ta bring him down hard."

"You're saying I'm jealous of him and her?"

"Yep."

"Well, I'm not."

"It sure seems like it ta me," the marshal said, glaring at Jared. "Cole Zanuck is an upstandin' citizen, an' you think bringin' him down will make the Doc come a-runnin' ta you. Is thet it?"

"No, that's not it. It's about right and wrong, about justice," Jared shot back. "That's our job, isn't it, justice?

And if you believe Jim Derby left town and just disappeared from the face of the earth, you're crazy as a loon!"

Jared's words hit the marshal like a cold rain, cooling him down some. He sat speechless for a few moments. "Damn if you ain't somethin', Jared. Yer a rare bird, you are. I sure hate ta lose you. I sure do. I was hopin' ta retire in a year an' have you take over. This town needs someone like you."

"Maybe they do," Jared replied, "but they sure don't want me around anymore."

"If it was my say, I'd keep you, Jared. I'm plumb sorry things took a turn like this. You got the makin's of a mighty fine lawman."

"Thanks Marshal," Jared replied. "You're a damn good marshal, and you've got my respect." They shook hands.

The next day, Lauren and Cole Zanuck left in his private, two-horse coach with his two bodyguards up front in the driver's box. They headed north for Atwood City where he would meet with his big-town lawyers who had managed to finagle a judge's trial.

They had gathered numerous statements attesting that Zanuck had acted in self-defense and that the cowboy had come at him with a boot knife. The knife in question was in the hands of Zanuck's lawyers and taken to the trial in a sealed box as evidence. They made sure there was no doubt as to the innocence of the accused, who was one of Rattlesnake Flat's most prominent and upstanding citizen, who contributed to the town's welfare.

All this commotion cost Cole Zanuck money, a lot of money. Especially the promise of a large contribution to the Judge's next election campaign, a deal made through Zanuck's lawyers.

A day after Lauren and Zanuck left for Atwood City, the town gave Miss Ella a fancy burial next to her husband up on the hillside behind her white frame house.

Uriah Freed built her a fine pine box with flower designs cut into the wood and gave it two coats of shellac. A small caravan of buckboards rolled slowly out of town and along the road to her place ten miles away. A little boy sat next to the driver on the buckboard that carried her casket and beat a slow dirge on a drum all the way to her place.

The grave had already been dug the day before by a crew of volunteers. A sturdy pine headboard stood a few feet behind it, engraved with Miss Ella's name and the dates of her coming and going in this life. The heavenly powers saw to it that the sun was bright and the air was clear and warm, just for Miss Ella.

Uriah Freed, as he did on rare occasions if the deceased was important enough, read from the Bible. A young rancher's daughter sang "Amazing Grace" a cappella as four cowboys lowered Miss Ella slowly into Mother Earth. After the hole was filled in and flowers were placed on the grave, everyone rounded up the loose pigs and chickens and took them home.

When everyone left and the quiet set back in, the old hound dog came out of the woods, scratched itself behind the ears and laid across Miss Ella's grave to sleep.

Somehow, Rattlesnake Flats didn't seem the same without her.

After Miss Ella's passing was eulogized in an editorial in the *Rattlesnake Flats Gazette*, many people came to lay claim on what was left of her land and property, which wasn't much. There wasn't much left because when her husband died and things began to unravel for her, Miss Ella started selling off large parcels to the ranchers. What was once a multi-acre farm had, over the years, been reduced to just five acres of land.

Of course, each claim was exposed as a fake. Miss Ella's little piece of heaven lay intestate. Not even the town, or anyone in town, could lay claim on it. It all sat there, house, barn and land, ten miles from Rattlesnake Flats, a silent monument to a great woman.

9.

A day after Miss Ella's funeral, Jared got real nosey and started sniffing around town. He sniffed through the fields and pine stands near Rattlesnake Flats, looking for any sign that signified a grave being dug. He even checked the back alleys and old barns, anywhere he thought a body could be stashed.

Jared also asked a lot of questions. This annoyed some of the townspeople and they complained to the mayor, Otis Jensen. He, in turn, complained to Marshal Nelson.

The marshal took Jared aside. "Look here, now, Jared," he whined, "maybe ya best slack off a bit. Yer pullin' the cinch a bit too tight an' people are startin' ta squawk."

Jared sighed and said, "I'm about out of ideas, anyway, Marshal."

"Didn't I tell ya it was a waste a-time?"

"Yeah."

"Ya can't git water from a dry well when there ain't nothin in it. Any fool knows thet."

Jared's eye's perked up. "What Marshal?"

"Didn't I tell you there wasn't nothin' ta find?"

"I mean before you said that."

"Oh, about the dry well? It's an ol' gold miner's sayin'."

"But, that's it!" Jared yelled. "Isn't there an old, dry well out behind the Bar Z Saloon? Back near the woods?"

The marshal gave Jared a skeptical stare. "Yeah, there is. What about it?"

"Has anyone checked it out for a dead body?"

"It's got a heavy wood cover nailed on it so no kids or drunks kin fall in it. There ain't no dead body in it, if thet's what yer a-thinkin'."

"Are you sure? Would you swear to that?"

The marshal shook his head. "Darn it, Jared, you jest won't give up on it, will ya? Yer like a damn bulldog. Ya get yer teeth inta somethin' and ya jest won't let it go! Yer causin' me a lot of headaches with the mayor and the town. I hope ya know thet!"

Jared chuckled. He saw the strange look on the marshal's face. It was a look that said he half believed Jared.

"You're not sure, are you, Marshal? You're thinking the same as I am. There is no way that Jim Derby would sell a thriving business to Cole Zanuck. And he wouldn't leave the town he loved without saying goodbye to anyone. Even if he did, he'd tell his friends, at least."

"If what you say is true, it all don't mean a thing without Jim Derby's body!"

"No, it doesn't," Jared admitted.

But he knew he had sown the seeds of doubt in the marshal's mind. All he had to do was wait. And it didn't take long.

"Alright, alright! We'll take a look at thet darn well, damn it! Git yer rope!"

The marshal fished a pry bar out of the desk drawer, grabbed the oil lamp off his desk and walked outside. Jared got his lariat from his saddle and followed close, smiling.

"I feel like a damn fool," the marshal muttered. He went past people without so much as a nod or a greeting.

"You'll feel better later," Jared chuckled.

The marshal pretended not to hear him and kept walking with a bothered look on his face. They soon came to an alley that circled around behind the Bar Z Saloon. In the field behind the saloon was a large rain barrel on a trestle.

"Jim Derby had thet rain barrel built right after the well went dry," the marshal told Jared. "He needed a ready supply of water fer the saloon."

"Where's the well?" Jared asked.

"Over there in the bushes." The marshal pointed to a cluster of vines and tall weeds. They walked over to it, forced their way through the dense vegetation and found the well.

It had a square wooden box around it, about three feet high, made of heavy wood. A sturdy plank cover was nailed to the box.

The marshal handed Jared the pry bar. "You do it. I'll jest stand here an git ready ta say I told ya so."

Jared took the pry bar, jammed its head under the edge of the cover and pried downward. The old lid groaned and creaked and finally started to give way. Jared got it high enough so that he could work his way completely around it inch by inch. In less than an hour they were able to lift the lid and flip it over the side onto the ground.

Jared lit the oil lamp, tied one end of the lariat to the handle and lowered it into the dark hole.

"How deep is it?"

"Fifteen, maybe twenty feet," the marshal replied.

They leaned over the side as Jared slowly lowered the oil lamp into the well. It took a long time before they saw something far below. When the lamp was about five feet from the bottom they saw the skeletal remains of a body. Nothing else was left, except for a few shreds of rag and bone.

"There he is!"

The marshal said, "We don't know fer sure. It kin be anybody."

Jared realized the old man was right. It was a body, but now the question was, whose body was it? Jim Derby or someone else?

Suddenly the marshal said, "Derby was a widower. He wore a gold band with his wife's name cut into it."

Jared sighed. For a moment he'd just about given up hope. Now he had it again. "I'm going down there," Jared said.

"We'll need help. I'll git Tom Sloan the blacksmith and his helper, Jim Sweeny. They got a lot a rope, too."

After the marshal left, Jared tied his lariat to a nail sticking out of the wooden box, leaving the lamp hanging down in the hole. He rolled a cigarette and smoked while he thought of why he was doing all this.

Was it for Lauren Goodwin, or was it because he resented being a lowly twenty-dollar a month deputy while Zanuck was a handsome, successful businessman with money, a man the town respected more than him? After all, they had tossed him aside because Zanuck had told them to.

He was finished smoking by the time the marshal returned with the blacksmith, his helper and a coil of rope.

"Who's the lightest?' Tom Sloan asked.

"I guess that's me," Jared replied.

Sloan, a big man with arms as round as Jared's legs, tied the heavy rope around Jared's chest, just below his armpits. "Don't worry, Jared," Sloan chuckled. "We won't drop ya."

Sloan and Sweeny took hold of the rope as Jared climbed over the side of the box and down into the well.

"Jest yell out when yer there," Sloan said.

"Okay!"

"Watch out fer the snakes!" Sweeny hollered. Then, "Jest kiddin', Jared. It's the big spiders ya gotta watch out fer!"

"Shut up, Sweeny," the marshal said, "or it's yer big ass that'll be goin' down instead of Jared's!"

They lowered the rope slowly, listening for a signal from Jared.

"You okay, Jared?" the marshal shouted into the well.

"Yeah, so far. Had to kill a few of those spiders Sweeny was talking about."

It went like that for a few minutes, talking back and forth, until Jared shouted back. "Okay! I'm down!"

The men on top stared down into the shadowy deepness of the well. They could barely see a hint of dull light that was the oil lamp. At times it disappeared as Jared bent over it. They heard his heavy breathing echoing up the well shaft.

After a while they heard Jared laughing hard.

The old marshal chuckled and said, "Well, I'll be go to hell! He found Jim Derby! Kiss my butt!"

10.

The following day the marshal requested a meeting with the mayor and members of the town council. They met at Della's Place over coffee and pie at a table in a far corner. The marshal took Jared with him.

The marshal put Jim Derby's ring on the table for all to see. Mr. Milner, the publisher of the *Gazette*, picked it up and closely inspected it. "Yes, it's Jim Derby's ring, alright. There's no doubt about that."

Gil Baxter, the mercantile owner, stared at Marshal Nelson. "You say you found it on a skeleton down in the old well behind the Bar Z Saloon, Marshal?"

"Jared did, yes. Tom Sloan will back us up on thet," the marshal replied.

Uriah Freed, the undertaker, took the ring from Milner and looked at it. He nodded. "Poor Jim. We were close friends. Before he disappeared, he told me he had his eye on Doc Goodwin. He wanted to marry her."

"He was interested in Doctor Goodwin?" Jared asked.

"Oh, sure," Freed replied. "The whole town knew Jim liked her. We all figured he was going to go further with it and ask her to marry him. He'd had enough of being a widower."

"Was Zanuck aware of Jim Derby's intentions?" Jared asked.

"Sure," Freed added. "They both made a fuss over her."

Gil Baxter cut in with, "Zanuck offered to buy the Bar D from Jim right off the bat, but Jim always said no. Zanuck must have changed Jim's mind, somehow."

The marshal cleared his throat for attention. "Ah, Jared here has the notion thet Zanuck murdered Jim Derby an' dumped his body down the well."

Gil Baxter laughed nervously. "That's pretty hard to believe. After all, Cole Zanuck never showed any anger towards Jim. They were pretty respectful toward each other, right, Uriah?"

"They sure were, Gil. I can't say nothing bad about Zanuck. He always treated me well."

"Same with me," Art Milner said.

Mayor Jensen, who had said little but had listened closely, looked at Jared and asked, "What exactly would Mr. Zanuck's motive be, Deputy?" He didn't sound very friendly.

Jared paused to think. "I don't know, unless he wanted to get rid of any competition with Doctor Goodwin. Also, he wanted the Bar D pretty badly, if I understand right."

"I don't think he'd kill Jim over anything like that," Freed said. "No, not Zanuck. He's a gentleman through and through."

"Anybody could have killed Jim," Gil Baxter said. "I say we forget the whole matter. It happened years ago and there's no evidence pointing to Mr. Zanuck as I can see. So, it wouldn't be right to say he did it."

Freed and Milner nodded in agreement. There was an uneasy silence.

Mayor Jensen cleared his throat again and said, "We won't go accusing Mr. Zanuck of anything, Marshal. Is that understood?"

"Alright, Mayor," the marshal replied. "It's done with. Over."

The mayor stared at Jared. "Is that clear, Deputy?"

"Yes, sir," Jared said calmly.

"We'll bring Jim Derby's remains up and give him a decent burial," Otis Jensen said. "The bank will bear the cost. We'll bury his ring with him."

That was that, and the members of the Rattlesnake Flats town council got up and left Della Lang's beanery. Jared and the marshal stayed for another cup of coffee.

"Well, it was a try," Jared said. "I guess they're right. There's no way to prove Zanuck killed Derby short of a signed confession."

"An' maybe even thet wouldn't do it," the old marshal chuckled. "Zanuck walks on water in this town."

Della came over to their table. "They didn't pay for the coffee and pie, Marshal. I want them arrested!" she said jokingly.

"Don't worry, little darlin'," the marshal said. "I got it covered." He placed an eagle in her hand. Della kissed him on the cheek and walked off to talk to some customers.

"She likes you a lot, Marshal," Jared said.

"Now don't start that agin," the old marshal said. Jared laughed.

Not much happened and the end of the month came up. Jared turned in his deputy badge and collected his twenty dollars' pay.

He also got money from Tom Sloan on the sale of the three outlaw mustangs and from Gil Baxter on the sale of the rifles, saddles and other gear. Altogether, with the bounty money from the bank, he had two-thousand dollars hidden in his saddlebag's secret pocket.

"When ya leavin town, rich man?" the marshal chuckled.

"After I say adios to the Doc," Jared said. "Zanuck and her should be coming back any day now."

"Well, don't be in a big hurry," the marshal replied. He looked kind of lost. "I'll sure miss me an' you a-sittin' on the porch with our heels up on the railing, watchin' life go by and shootin' the bull."

"Yeah. So will I, Marshal."

"Yeah." The marshal nodded. "So will I, partner. I'll be here any time ya want ta come an' sit. It gits mighty lonesome sittin' here alone."

"Thanks, Marshal."

It was the first time he had called Jared his partner. The cowboy had gotten to like this new life of his and would miss it. But it was over now and there was nothing left, but to hit the trail.

The nice thing about sitting on the porch of the jail was that there was a clear view of the Doc's place on the other side of the street. Not a direct view, since it was down the road a bit, but good enough to see her come and go. It was for that very reason that Jared spent the next three days sitting there with the marshal. On day four, Zanuck's private coach pulled up with his two black-clad bodyguards on the driver's bench.

Jared watched Lauren quickly get out and rush into her place. The coach pulled away with Zanuck still in it. He had never even gotten out, as a gentleman should. The coach headed for the Bar Z and pulled around to the back where Zanuck had his quarters.

"Well, there she is, Jared," the marshal said. "Go say yer goodbyes."

Jared nodded. He suddenly realized this part of his life was about to end for good. The only thing left was to say farewell to this wonderful, brave woman. He stood up, glanced at the marshal, walked slowly across the street and went into Lauren's office. The reception room was empty. Someone was sobbing in the room where she did her work, so he walked quietly back there to take a look.

The sobbing suddenly stopped. He saw Lauren sitting in a chair, hunched over. On her head was a bonnet with a veil. The veil hung over her face. She gave a start when Jared walked over to her. As she looked up, he slowly and gently lifted the veil over the brim of her hat.

He saw that her face very badly bruised.

"What happened?" he asked. He already knew the answer.

"He's no gentleman. Jared," she said haltingly. Her voice was filled with pain and sadness.

Jared's eyes narrowed into fiery slits.

"I'm sorry to hear that," he said. "Is there anything I can do?"

"No," Lauren said. "If I could just be alone right now, I would appreciate it very much."

"Alright, then. Get some rest," Jared said softly, trying to sound calm. He left.

Out on the street he checked his Colt, then walked over to the jail. The marshal was inside looking through some wanted fliers. He looked up as Jared came in.

"You look like yer goodbye didn't go too well. What happened?"

"He beat her."

"Who? Zanuck?"

"Yes. I think he tried to take her."

The marshal stood up. He stared at Jared, his eyes narrow with smoldering rage. "I'll kill the s-o-b," he growled.

"You can kill him after I do," Jared said calmly.

Suddenly the marshal calmed down. "We'll have to go through his bodyguards," he said.

"Not you, me," Jared said. "It's my play, old man."

"Stick thet old man crap up yer ass, sonny-boy! It time ta separate Mr. Zanuck from his nursemaids."

The marshal checked his Colt. He and Jared went out to find Zanuck.

As they walked down the street towards the Bar Z Saloon, Mr. Milner and Mayor Jensen came out of the *Gazette* and walked in their direction. They came together in front of the newspaper office.

"What's up, Marshal?" Milner asked. "You look angry about something."

"Thet sidewinder, Zanuck, was disrespectful ta the Doc," the marshal said, "an' I'm gonna spank his ass good!"

Milner looked at the mayor. Mayor Jensen frowned at the lawman.

"Now, let's not be hasty, Marshal," Jensen said. "The town doesn't want any trouble with Mr. Zanuck.

Jared cut in. "Zanuck tried to forced himself on Miss Goodwin. He violated the code."

"Well, perhaps, but the code isn't a written law," Jensen said, "and it can't be enforced by the law. I'm sorry, but that's how it is. Miss Goodwin will have to press charges if she wants satisfaction, Jared."

His tone of voice said that Jared was nothing but a stupid, uneducated cowboy.

"You wouldn't say that if you saw the bruises on Miss Goodwin's face, Mayor," Jared said.

"What? He hit her?" Milner asked.

"Yes," Jared said. "I saw her face."

"Ta hell with talkin' to these two assholes, Jared," the marshal growled. "Let's go!"

They walked off leaving the mayor and Milner slack-jawed and confused.

"I'm warning you, Marshal!" Mayor Jensen yelled. "You work for me!"

"Not any more I don't!" The marshal stopped long enough to rip off his badge and toss it up the road at the mayor.

He and Jared walked down towards the Bar Z Saloon.

11.

Jared and the old marshal walked cautiously up the steps and stood on the porch of the saloon. They listened a moment as a dog barked up the road by the bank. Finally, they adjusted their gunbelts, looking at each other.

Not far away, Milner and Jensen stood watching them as they went through the batwing doors.

There were only a few customers at that early hour. Zanuck stood leaning on the bar as he talked to the barman about something.

His two bodyguards were sitting at a table near the wall. One was looking through a copy of the *Rattlesnake Flats Gazette* while the other was playing solitaire. When they saw Jared and the marshal, they stopped doing what they were doing and stared at them, watching their every move with keen interest.

When Jared saw Zanuck's two men, he put some open space between him and the marshal, letting his right hand hang down by his holster.

"What can I do for you, Marshal Nelson?" Zanuck asked, as if he were annoyed by the interruption.

"You kin come over to the jailhouse," the marshal said.

Zanuck glanced over at his guards to make sure they were paying attention. "I'd like to, but I'm a little busy right now."

Zanuck saw that the marshal wasn't wearing his badge.

"Where's your badge, Marshal?"

"Forgit thet. Jest come along an' there'll be no trouble."

Zanuck laughed. "Trouble? Am I in trouble, Marshal?"

"I'm only gonna say it one more time, Zanuck," the marshal said calmly. "Let's go!"

Zanuck's two guards got up and started to move forward. Jared stepped in front with his back to Zanuck, blocking him from their view.

"Move aside, cowboy," the tall one growled, "before you get yer ass whipped."

Jared stood there, a half of a smile on his lips as the few customers got up and rushed outside.

"You boys best sit down," Jared said. "This doesn't concern either of you. It's the marshal's official business."

Zanuck's two guards smirked.

"We don't take orders from assholes like you, cowboy!" the short one growled. "So, move aside or get hurt."

"Sit down or draw," Jared said.

As Zanuck's gunnies drew, Jared stepped to his left and crouched low. He fanned four quick shots off so fast it almost sounded like a cannon's roar.

Zanuck's guards were a hair too slow and a bit too confident. A fusillade of lead smacked into their bodies and sent them flying against the wall. Their shots went wild, hitting the ceiling and floor. They bounced off the wall, scattered some tables and toppled over, face down in a heap.

As Jared quickly began to reload, the marshal shouted.

"Jared! Watch out!"

Zanuck had pulled his derringer and let go with a snap shot. It went too high and grazed the side of Jared's head, taking his hat off, sending it flying across the room.

The marshal's gun barked as its bullet slammed into Zanuck's chest, sending him spinning along the bar. For a moment Zanuck smiled, but the smile slowly faded as he slipped down into a sitting position on the floor.

"You rotten old sonofabitch!" Zanuck muttered.

Those were his last words. His head dropped down on his chest and he rolled sideways, upsetting a spittoon and staring blankly up at the ceiling with a puzzled look on his face.

"Jesus!" the barman said after coming up for air behind the bar. "You jest put me out of a job, Marshal!"

"Hell," the marshal chuckled. "You jest got a promotion ta manager, sonny!"

Jared walked over and picked his hat off the floor.

"You alright, Jared?" the marshal asked.

"Not so much."

"Yer bleedin'. You'd best go let the Doc look at it."

"Yeah, I'll do that."

"You go on. I'll take care of this mess."

Mayor Jensen, Milner and a lot of townspeople came rushing into the saloon. Jared ignored them and left.

With his hat in his hand, Jared cut through the crowd and went slowly up the road to the Doc's place. She was standing on the porch without her bonnet, shading her eyes. She saw the blood on the left side of Jared's face.

She grabbed his arm, took him into the back room and sat him down. "Who shot you? His guards?"

"No," Jared said. "Zanuck ambushed me."

"Why?"

"Because he felt like it, I guess."

"Be serious."

"Alright. The marshal and I tried to arrest him."

"Because of me?"

Jared didn't answer. She cupped his face in her two hands.

"Answer me, Jared! Was it because of me?"

"Maybe."

Before he realized it, she had bent and kissed him softly on the lips. She held it a while, pulled back and tapped him lightly on the end of his nose with one finger.

"You're a bad boy," she said.

"I know," he said softly, still off balance from the kiss.

12.

With Cole Zanuck dead, Rattlesnake Flats slowly settled down into a comfortable status quo. The town took ownership of the Bar Z Saloon and hired the barman, Bob Clark, to stay on as manager with the option to buy.

Mayor Jensen pinned the badge back on Marshal Nelson and offered Jared his deputy job back. Jared said he'd think it over.

The town also took ownership of Miss Ella's parcel of land and put it up for sale.

Jared realized that his life as a cowboy had come to an end. The big freeze of a year ago had changed the cattle business forever. It would need time to come back again, and when it did, it would be smaller and smarter, with better stock.

In the meantime, cowboys went around looking for jobs. Many headed south, from Kansas into Texas, or north into Nebraska and Montana, begging for work. Most didn't own a horse or a saddle anymore, having sold them for whiskey money or a place to sleep.

Many cowboys hit the outlaw trail to rob banks and trains. Jared, though, was in a good position. He had a horse, a rig and over two thousand dollars deposited in the Rattlesnake Flats Savings and Loan.

He hung out on the jailhouse porch with the marshal, thinking about how best to leave Rattlesnake Flats, but really not wanting to go. There was no reason to rush off and look for a job anymore. He'd rather be near the Doc. She was still learning the ways of the West and he wanted to keep an eye on her. Nothing intimate.

At least that's what he told himself.

One day Jared and the marshal were sunning their heels on the jailhouse porch railing when the marshal got personal.

"Whatta ya gonna do about her, Jared?" the marshal asked bluntly.

"About who?" Jared pretended he didn't know who the marshal was taking about.

"The Doc."

"I'm not in a position to do anything about her."

"Well, I got the feelin' she's a-waitin' fer you ta make a move on her."

Jared only shrugged and said nothing.

The old man went on. "Don't make the same mistake I did, Jared. I once had the chance ta marry the sweetest girl in the world. Instead, I rode off and left her. I still regret it."

The old man stopped talking to stare at Jared for a moment.

"An' this town thinks a lot of you, too, Jared. You came in here an' saved its bacon, an' they know it. Ya cleared up thet Jim Derby mess, too."

"I must admit I do feel comfortable here," Jared replied.

"This town ain't finished yet. It's gonna grow. Someday the ranchers an' the cowboys will come inta town agin ta git drunk and spend money. It'll be like old days agin."

Jared chuckled. "Yeah, and sure as heck, one day a bunch will ride in and rob the bank, too."

The marshal shrugged. He stared hard at Jared. "They want you back as deputy real bad."

"It looks like it."

"So, whatta ya gonna do, Jared? Ride off an' leave? Don't do it, boy. Stay here, take thet deputy job an' marry the Doc."

Jared looked tortured. "I don't know. I'd best move on."

"So, yer not stayin, then?"

"I don't think so," Jared said. "I ain't the kind to settle down. I guess I've been a cowboy too long."

"You gotta do somethin' meaningful with yer life, Jared, "Ya can't jest waste it or throw it away."

"Maybe I'll go through those wanted fliers and posters you get on the mail stage."

The marshal looked at Jared with a surprised look on his face. "You're gonna be a bounty hunter?"

"I'm thinking about it."

"Are you serious? Ya wanna put yer life on the line every day like thet? You got tha itch fer danger that bad?"

"I can do it. You already saw that."

The old man shook his head. "Yer making the mistake of yer life, Jared. You better give it some thought."

"I already have."

"Take my advice, Jared. Marry the Doc, buy Miss Ella's place an' take the deputy job. Next year you kin be marshal an' I'll retire."

"I'll give it some thought, Marshal." Jared replied.

Two days later Jared decided to leave. He had the fliers for several wanted men in his secret saddlebag pocket along with some money, food, supplies and ammo for his Colt and his rifle.

"The Doc told me she wants ta check out yer wound, Jared," the marshal said.

"It's fine. She's checked it out twice already."

"Well, jest humor her. Go over there. She waitin' fer ya."

He hadn't planned on saying goodbye. Goodbyes were messy. He'd be seeing her when he got back, if and when he ever did.

"Alright, I'll go."

"Don't forget. She's expectin' you." The marshal suddenly gave Jared a soulful look. His eyes were moist. "Damn it! You take care, sonny! Don't turn yer back on nobody, ya hear?"

Marshal Aaron Nelson gave Jared a big hug, something he'd never done before.

"Hell, don't get all choked up, old man. I'll be back one of these days."

Jared went outside, grabbed the reins of his horse and walked it across the street to the Doc's place. He tied it to the rail and went in. Lauren was reading a medical book. She looked up at him.

"My wound is fine, Doc."

"I know. It's not that."

"He told you?"

She put the book down and stood up, facing him.

"Don't do it, Jared. Please!"

Jared saw the concern on her face. For a moment he was ready to stay, but pushed the feeling aside. He wanted to grab her in his arms, but couldn't find the will to do it.

"I can't cowboy any more, Doc. Those days are over."

She looked about to cry.

"Then stay on as a deputy. They want you."

Jared shrugged. Lauren put a hand on his arm and came close.

He looked down into her eyes as she stared up into his. He wanted to kiss her badly but knew if he did, it would be all over. He would be stuck here forever. He would no longer be a cowboy. He'd have to bury that part of him.

Jared forced himself to pull back.

"Promise me you'll come back, Jared," she said.

"I will, I promise, Doc."

He kissed her lightly on the cheek to end it and left.

She followed him out, watching him mount up. The marshal stood on the porch of the jailhouse looking across the street at them. As Jared rode away, the marshal waved at him but Jared was slumped over his horse, looking the other way. He never even noticed.

Jared kept riding, afraid to look back for fear of choking up. He fought back the stinging in his eyes. The thought of leaving Lauren Goodwin forever bit into him. He wanted to stay and he wanted to go. The conflict was killing him. He started to turn back.

"No!" he said to himself and kept riding.

He rode west along the road. About ten miles on, for some reason, he made a left turn off the coach road and onto the trail that led to Miss Ella's place. He didn't know why. It was as if something was pulling him in that direction.

Five miles more, he came over a rise. He stopped to look down at the deserted white two-story frame house and the big red barn where the party had taken place. For a moment he thought he saw Miss Ella on the porch waving to him. He blinked his eyes, it wasn't her but Lauren Goodwin. When he blinked again she too was gone.

Was it a vison, a glimpse of something to come?

It seemed strange that no one was living there anymore. The house was empty, the barn was empty, everything was empty.

Slowly he rode down toward the yard. It seemed to be the right thing to do.

"Thirsty, old pal?" Jared said to the horse. "Let's go get a drink."

Once in the yard, he dismounted and stood looking around. He had a warm feeling inside. His horse went over to the water trough by the windmill and began sucking up water. When it was finished, it walked down to the barn by itself.

Jared watched it go, chuckled and walked up on the porch. After a few moments, he went inside to look around. The house seemed to welcome him. Maybe it was Miss Ella's spirit. He thought he could feel her presence, her warmth.

He stood in the hallway. "Hi, Miss Ella," Jared said out loud. His voice echoed off the barren walls.

Jared chuckled again, wondering what he was doing there. It wasn't in his plans. He walked into the kitchen and stared at the big cast iron stove, table and chairs. The place needed to be lived in, brought back to life. If not, it would wither and die.

Jared went back out on the porch to roll a cigarette. Then stopped. Half a mile down the road he saw something moving. As it came closer he saw it was someone in a buckboard. That someone soon became Lauren Goodwin.

She pulled up and stopped in the yard. He ran eagerly to her and helped her down.

"What are you doing here, Clay?" she asked.

Suddenly he said, "I'm thinking of buying the place, Doc." He didn't know why he said it, but once the words were out he was glad he had.

"Really?"

"Yup. So, what are you doing here?"

"After you left, I felt the urge to take a ride. It kind of came over me all of a sudden."

"Yeah. I know that feeling."

"What about that other thing? Are you still going away?"

"I don't think so. As I see it now, maybe it wasn't such a good idea."

"So you changed your mind, did you? Just like that?"

He shrugged. "I've been giving it some more thought."

"So, you're going to buy Miss Ella's place?"

"Yeah. I think she would like that."

"Are you serious?"

"Yup. I sure am," Jared answered, staring back at the house.

"What are you going to do with it?"

"Live in it, I reckon. Grow some roots."

"All alone? It's kind of big for one person, isn't it?"

"Yeah, but I figured it'd be about right for two people." He walked up close, looking down at her.

"What two people? You have someone else in mind, do you?"

"Yeah. You. Me. The two of us."

"Did you say the two of us? You and me?"

"I guess I did, didn't I?" He seemed surprised at himself.

She glanced across the yard at the windmill for a moment, then turned to stare up at him. "Can you say it in another way?"

"Sure," Jared said. He looked down at his boots for a moment, to get his words in line. Finally, he blurted out, "Will you marry me, Doc?"

She laughed and smiled. "It took some doing, didn't it?"

"Yeah. I guess the cowboy in me was fighting it. But not anymore."

"Do you love me, Clay?"

"Yes."

"Then, yes, I'll marry you."

"I'm honored, ma'am." He took her in his arms and kissed her.

The old hound dog came around the corner of the house to greet them and have its back scratched.

"Here's our best man," Jared chuckled.

Lauren replied, "We'll have to get him a coat and tie." They both broke out laughing.

They walked up to the porch, sat down on the steps and looked out on the field of sunflowers and bush clover beyond the yard. High above, an eagle floated effortlessly on the wind. Jared looked up at it and chuckled.

Lauren held his arm tight. "Tell him you're not going."

Jared looked up. "No," he said. "I'm stayin' here."

They moved close and held on for fear of losing each other.

Soon the eagle was gone.

The End

A Note from the Author

Thank you for reading my book. Would you please consider rating and reviewing it? I'd enjoy your feedback. Thank you!

Western Books by R. Annan

Fight for the Lazy M

The Gunfighter in Winter

Long Ride to Hell's Kitchen

Owl Hawks

Gunfight at Barfield Springs

Shootout at Sanctuary City

Last Days of a Gunfighter

The Red Bandana

Copperhead Moon

Cowboys of the Box R

Prisoners of Brimstone Pass

Range War in C Minor

Devil Wind

Showdown at Wamego Falls

Lightning Riders

Winter Kill

Look for other western books to appear soon.

About the Author

R. Annan is a well-traveled author with many interests. As a career serviceman, he served in Korea and Vietnam. He also completed a one-year course at the Defense Language Institute in Monterey, California, and graduated from the University of South Florida with a B.A. in Art and Art History. After taking a two-year course in screenwriting at the Hollywood Scriptwriting Institute, he established The Old Time Radio Club Time Machine as both a scriptwriter and an actor.

As a young boy growing up in the city, R. Annan never passed up a chance to see a Western movie. His heroes were Buck Jones, Johnny Mack Brown, Wild Bill Elliot and John Wayne, to name a few. As an adult, he often wondered where his love of Westerns came from. Perhaps it has something to do with his grandfather, John L. Annan, who was a cowboy from Helena, Montana, in days of old.